USA *Today* Bestselling Author

Dale Mayer

TERKEL'S TEAM SERIES

BRODY'S BEAST

BOOK 07

BRODY'S BEAST: TERKEL'S TEAM, BOOK 7
Beverly Dale Mayer
Valley Publishing Ltd.

ISBN-13: 978-1-773365-27-5
Print Edition

Books in This Series:

About This Book

Welcome to a brand-new series from *USA Today* best-selling author Dale Mayer, where dark-ops SEALs have special senses and skills, needed to solve intrigue, betrayal, and … murder. A series with all the elements you've come to love, plus so much more, … including psychics!

The journey back to consciousness hadn't been fast or easy but, once awake, with weird images and voices in his head, Brody is all about getting back to the team and into the action. His senses are dulled, but, even then, he's strong enough to know he has to leave the building where he's been recuperating from the initial team accident. Not knowing any of the details doesn't help, but it does mean trust is now the issue.

Clary came on board to help when Brody was lost on the ethers—and to help her sister, Cara, who had taken on more than she could handle with Rick's care. And even though Clary had been forewarned as to how this type of connection could work, Clary didn't expect it to work with her and her patient, Brody.

Having a healing pathway was one thing; … having a connection where you could hear thoughts, feel the same emotions, was quite another. And seeing how Brody fights to surmount the attacks on the team he loves so well only shows her how much more is possible—but not the event where she must test out her theory, … unless it's to protect those she cares about.

PROLOGUE

*B*RODY?

He shuddered.

Brody came the insistent voice yet again.

He tried to block it out. It had been yelling and screaming at him for what seemed like forever. He'd done everything he could to make it go away, but still it was persistent. He tried once again to shut it down, but it came back once more.

No, not this time came the calm voice. *We need you. Get up, get out, come back.*

Brody thought it was Terk's voice. He wasn't sure, but maybe? It was hard to tell what Terk's problem was.

But, if Terk called, it meant that he needed something. And, if Terk needed something, Brody would be there for him. Except how could he be sure it was Terk?

It didn't really sound like him; it seemed a long distance away. And then he heard that woman's voice again. "Who the hell was that?" Again came the softer voice.

Come on, Brody. Wake up. Come on. It's time to wake up. You've had a nice nap, but that time is over.

He sighed and twisted. He wanted to sleep some more. He wanted to tell them that he was still too tired and that he still needed sleep, but he didn't think they would care. He tried to block them out yet again, but the male voice returned, insistent and hard.

No, that's enough now. Come out now, on your own, or come out with our help.

Brody slowly opened his eyes, only to see nothing. It was just black out there. He snapped his eyelids closed again. "See? I tried," he muttered.

The female laughed. *Oh no you don't. You don't get off so easy*, she murmured. *Try it again.*

"No."

Yes.

"No."

Yes. And I'm glad to see you've got enough strength to argue, Terk said telepathically.

Brody froze. "Terk?"

Yeah, bud. We'd sure like to see you come back out of where you've been hiding.

"Hiding?" he snapped. Struggling higher and higher through the fog, he fought. How dare Terk say Brody was hiding? He'd never hidden in his life. He always took every fight head-on. There was no hiding in his life. Ever.

When he slowly drifted higher and higher, he looked around. "Where am I?" he cried out, feeling the first vestiges of fear. "It's dark."

And this time, the woman's voice, with something almost recognizable about it, soothed him. *We're here*, she stated. *We're waiting for you.*

He felt relief at hearing her voice again, but it was couched in a near panic because he didn't know who she was or where she was. "Where am I?" he asked, his voice almost strangled.

You've been in a coma, she stated calmly. *And we need you to come back now.*

"And if I don't want to?" he asked almost bitterly.

Too bad, she murmured. *You need to. Unless, of course, you continue to hide.*

He twisted, surging higher and higher again. "I don't hide," he growled, a darkness in his soul overriding everything that they were doing. "I don't know who you are or why you would say that to me," he snapped, "but I don't hide."

Then suddenly it looked like he was … here. He opened his eyes and saw a room. Relief washed through him. It wasn't just darkness. It wasn't a never-ending unwavering blackness surrounding him. As he fully opened his eyes, he looked around. He was in a room, a small bedroom. And he was alone. "Where am I?" he whispered.

You're safe, a woman said quietly. *And I need you to stay safe. All your friends are about to be attacked, and so are you.*

He struggled to toss off all the cloudiness and a bit of fog in his brain. "I don't understand," he muttered. "Where are you?"

I'm here, she stated calmly. *You can talk to me anytime.*

Just then a woman walked into his room. She stopped, looked at him, and smiled. "There you are," she greeted him.

He frowned. *The voice is different.* "You sound surprised."

"Sure," she replied. "I wasn't expecting to see you awake."

He looked at her hard. "Who were you expecting to see?"

She shrugged. "Good question, but not you. I thought you were a goner."

"Well, I'm not," Brody snapped, his tone harsh. "Where are the rest of my friends?"

"They're around," she said. "I'll call the doc."

"No doctor," Brody muttered. "I'm fine." And he slowly

sat up.

"No, no, no, you don't," she cried out in alarm.

He glared and ignored her. "I'm getting up," he declared, "and I don't think you are capable of stopping me." Then that voice, the one from his psyche, the one that kept talking to him, the one that called him home, whispered to him.

What about me though? she asked. *I am capable of stopping you.*

He looked around in alarm. "Who said that?"

The nurse looked at him in surprise. "Nobody said anything," she noted cautiously, frowning at him. "That's just a sign that you're not quite back with us yet," she murmured. "Please relax."

He shook his head. "That's not happening," he argued, as he managed to get his legs over the side of the bed. But he was weak; damn, he was weak. He glared as he looked around at the room. "Where am I?"

The nurse looked at him. "I'll call Terk."

"You do that. And tell him to bring me some damn clothes."

And, with that, she took off.

The voice in his head laughed. *Cute,* she said. *You're worrying about your hairy butt after everything you've been through?*

He frowned. "Who the hell are you, and how do you know I've got a hairy butt?"

Because I've seen it, she teased cheerfully. *It's kind of cute too. We'll talk when I get there.*

"No," Brody argued. "I don't know who you are or what you're doing, but my team is in trouble. I have to go to them. So, if you want to talk, it'll wait until afterward."

CHAPTER 1

SOMETHING HIT BRODY and hit him hard. It was like an unseen force, sapping all the strength out of him. Brody collapsed back on the bed.

"I don't know what the hell just happened," he said out loud. He knew no one was in the room, but the question was more to himself than anyone else. He knew he was alone, yet …

"If somebody did this to me, … you'll pay for it." He tried to inject a serious threat into his tone. The conviction was evident, and, if anyone was out there at all, they had to know he wasn't kidding. And he wasn't.

He didn't know what the hell was going on, but that voice in his head was beyond scary.

You shouldn't ever be scared of the voices in your head, the woman stated calmly. *I'm only here to help.*

By knocking me out?

If you get up and run too quickly, she noted, *you'll knock yourself out.*

I guess I'll learn then, won't I?

Ah! Stubborn, aren't you?

Independent, he argued.

After a moment of silence, she continued. *Fine, now try it again.*

He groaned as he pushed himself up, but now it felt like

he had weights around his ankles and his chest, all holding him down. *I don't understand. Why does everything feel like it's so far away? So heavy?*

Because you've been in a coma for a long time, she explained in exasperation. *Do you remember me telling you that?*

Sure, you might have told me, but that doesn't mean I necessarily believed you.

She snorted. *Of course not. I mean, why would you listen to anybody, especially anyone who is trying to help? Are you always this obnoxiously stubborn?*

He almost smiled at that. *Probably.* After a moment of sitting upright, he said, *There. See? I'm doing much better.*

Sure you are, she quipped. *You do realize you're talking to yourself in your head, right?*

He frowned at that. *Aren't you the one who just told me that I shouldn't be afraid of the voices in my head?*

Sure, she agreed, *as long as you're comfortable with it.*

Well, I was comfortable, he noted in exasperation, *until now. Sounds like you're trying to put ideas in my head.*

Nope. … I just want to make sure that you don't do anything, too fast, and hurt yourself.

Now you sound like Terk and the rest of my team.

Good, she replied. *I imagine those guys care about your condition and are just looking out for you.*

Of course they are, but I also know that they need me. Something has gone wrong in our world, and I can't count on anybody.

That's sad, she murmured, *but I do understand.*

He frowned. *How do you know what it's like?* he asked, a note of challenge in his voice.

I didn't say I know what it's like, she corrected him, *but I do understand what it's like to not trust anyone around you.*

He nodded at that. *That experience is not just unique to our team, I'm sure.*

No, … and the minute you're different, people are scared of you, she noted, with the same sadness.

You mean, like this ability to talk to people in their heads?

That and being able to knock you out, if I need to. A flat edge filled her voice.

He believed her. She was formidable. He frowned. *I really would appreciate it if you didn't do that anymore.*

Don't be an idiot, she snapped. *And look after yourself, and I won't have to. I'm only here to help you and to keep you safe.*

He had to ponder that. *And that would mean that you know Terk.*

She laughed. *Yeah, I do. Although it's a bit more distant than that.*

That's confusing, he told her. *What do you mean?*

She hesitated. *It's really through my sister that I'm here.*

Okay. … So Terk didn't ask you to help me?

Terk asked my sister to help, she explained, *but I'm here instead.*

Your sister couldn't help?

She could, but it was also taking a lot out of her. You have to know that she's helping not just you. So I took over your care.

And the nurse out there?

It never hurts to have a physical representation of the medical profession, she noted, *even if we don't use them much.*

Oh, wow. So are you not a medical professional?

I am, she stated. *I'm a doctor but a fairly unusual one.*

In what way?

Because I do this kind of energy work, she explained. *My sister does it as well, but she's not a doctor.*

So, one trained and one not?

There's no formal training for stuff like this, she added, with a note of humor. *And you, of all people, should know that because you have very similar talents, if not necessarily in the same field.*

He struggled with that for a moment. *You know a lot about me, and that makes me uncomfortable.*

Yeah, I understand that, she agreed, *but really not a whole lot I can do to make you feel better about it. There are things that you need to do, things that you need to get a move on with, in order to keep everybody moving in your world.*

He frowned at that. *Are you deliberately trying to talk in circles?*

She groaned. *I don't know the circumstances around your team. I was hoping that you did because you seem so adamant.*

He was trying hard to follow her words. *I just know that I went down in unusual circumstances, and, now that I'm awake, I suspect that there are way more problems than I even know about.*

At that, another voice interrupted.

Clary, how is he doing?

He's doing better. Clary addressed Brody. *Meet Cara, my twin—well, triplet really, but our brother died.* Clary shifted her attention to her sister. *Cara, he's awake, but almost combative.*

Great. Cara gave a heavy sigh. *That just means he matches up with the rest of this group.*

Who's Cara to my team? Brody asked.

Well, you could say, I'm Rick's partner, she murmured gently. *He was in the same kind of situation as you are. I went in deep to try and save him, and then, when I came out, well, let's just say that we'd formed a bond that we hadn't really expected.*

It took a moment for Brody to digest it all. *Wow,* he murmured. *Is he okay?*

He's recovering nicely, and hopefully you will too. Everybody has been worried sick about you.

You've been in and out, Clary noted, *and, when Cara lost you in the ethers, it was pretty grim for a while.*

Thanks for that, Cara said, with a gasp. *Nothing like throwing me under the bus.*

Hey, that's what you told me, Clary stated. *If you want to rephrase, go ahead.*

Fine, Cara replied. *Brody, when you came looking for help, I was busy with Rick at the time and wasn't sure if you were a friend or foe.* She paused. *So I couldn't give you much more attention, while I was trying to keep Rick alive. Then, when I found out who you were and went back for you, I couldn't find you again.*

That's fine. Thanks for taking care of Rick. And I am here, aren't I? His voice was warming. *Rick and I are very good friends. I would never want you to prioritize me over him.* Brody hoped he sounded sincere because he meant it.

After a moment of silence, Cara laughed. *Well, he said something similar to me at one point as well, so apparently you guys are very much alike.*

We are, and, as long as he's doing okay, then I'm grateful, Brody stated, his tone more formal than he expected. But it was choking him up to think that Rick had been in the same kind of boat as he was. *What about the rest of my team?*

Well, you can talk to them yourself soon, Clary murmured. *Terk is on his way to you.*

He probably shouldn't do that, Brody stated in alarm. *I think our team is under attack.*

It is, and it has been for days, Cara agreed, *weeks, I guess. It's ugly, but you're the last one who needs to be brought back to full consciousness. You were lost for a while, which is one of the reasons I asked my sister to go fishing for you.*

Fishing, Brody repeated, tasting the word. *What an odd expression.*

Maybe, but it's what Clary does best, Cara added. *She's stronger than I am in some areas, particularly now that I'm much more connected to Rick.*

Well, it's a fascinating thing to talk about, and hopefully I'll get a chance to see you face-to-face and to thank you. At that moment, Brody heard noises in the other room. At almost the same time moment, the voices in his head blinked out. He frowned at that, hating the sensation of potentially losing some grasp on what was going on.

WHEN THE DOOR opened next, Terk strode toward him, a big grin on his face. "Now that's a sight for sore eyes." His arms outstretched, Terk came right next to Brody.

Brody gave him a weak smile but was eager to accept and to return the hug. "God, I feel like I've been run over by a full fleet of semis."

"You almost were," Terk admitted, "and, if it weren't for the talented women who have joined our team"—he seemed out of it for a second, then continued—"I don't think you would have survived."

"Well, if I was lost forever in that cold darkness," Brody stated, "I can tell you that's not a place that anybody wants to stay."

"Do you remember anything?"

"Not a whole lot." He studied Terk. "You look like you haven't been affected at all, and yet I feel like I've been gone for weeks, if not months."

"You have been," Terk agreed quietly. "I did get through the initial attack better than all of you," he added. "And I'm not even sure why necessarily, but finally now everybody but you is back on their feet."

"Everybody?" Brody needed to be sure, and, at his question, Terk hesitated.

"Well, almost everybody. Of our team, yes, all eight of us are back on our feet."

"Well, thank God for that," Brody murmured. And then he stopped. "So who didn't make it?"

"They attacked all three admins. Tasha was minorly injured and was able to hide until we found her. Wilson is dead, and Mera? … Well, she survived the first attack, though she was shot twice, but didn't know who could be trusted and so wouldn't come in. She was taken out when they came back around, while most everyone on the team was still comatose, and we were still trying to figure out what had happened."

"Good God," Brody asked, struggling with the bad news, "why would they take her out?"

"And Bob at the defense department, our contact there?"

"You mean, our ex-contact," Terk noted, his voice harsh.

It dawned on Brody. "He's dead."

Terk nodded. "Executed at the same time but claimed to be a heart attack. Even Lorelei was in a hit-and-run, but she survived." Terk sighed. "Exactly, our ex-contact. As you know, we were done and supposedly finished and officially disbanded, but then this happened."

"Did our government try to take us out and clean up

permanently in the process?"

"It's something we've been kicking around. It will take quite a bit to bring you back up to speed. A lot's going on," Terk stated, "and, I mean, *a lot*. One of the things you need to know is there have been follow-up attacks on multiple fronts. On nearly all of us and we have followed each attack back to one particular group. They're constantly cleaning up, exterminating their own ground forces, and, every time we turn around, hiring new footmen," he murmured. "It's frustrating because we're always one step behind. As soon as you're up for it, I'll give you a short synopsis."

At that, Brody shuffled up against the headboard, his body breaking out in a sweat. "Jesus, just even that much movement and I'm already exhausted."

"If you can let Cara give you a hand," Terk suggested, "you might get on your feet faster."

"Cara or Clary?" Brody asked.

Terk looked startled for a moment. "Is Clary here?"

"She's been keeping me sane on the other side," Brody murmured, "or as sane as it seems I can be."

At that, Terk whistled. "I'll have to ask Cara about that."

"Yeah, you do that," Brody noted. "I'm not exactly sure what's going on, but I do owe her my thanks. She was a beacon among all this."

"Yes, exactly," Terk agreed, "and, for that, we are most grateful to the whole group."

"I gather there are more involved than just our team?"

"Not just more, … a lot more," Terk murmured. "Let's start with Damon. He was up first."

BRODY SAT HERE in shock, as Terk ran down the whole story. "Good God, you need to get me out of here now."

At that, Terk smiled. "We're working on it, but you're not up to snuff, as you can tell."

"I know," he muttered, as he wiped the sweat off his face. "It's pretty distressing to be this weak. But to think that you guys have gone through so much already and are so shorthanded, with a big finale of some kind to come, I don't want to miss out."

Terk chuckled. "Of course you don't, as if you were likely to do that. The problem is, I can't have you be a vulnerability."

Terk was never one to pull his punches, and this was no different. But it really hurt when he said things like that to Brody. He stared at his old friend. "Well then, you need to find a way for me to get back on my feet and at your place, wherever the hell that is," he murmured.

"And amid all the attacks, we have established a temporary compound."

"Are we in England?" At Terk's nod, Brody snickered. "I bet MI6 doesn't appreciate that."

Terk snorted. "They would like to see us gone, no doubt. However, at the same time, these guys after us are now on MI6's turf and making a mess of their world. We're doing something to help MI6, so they're okay with that. But, yes, in the end, they want us gone."

"Have you thought about afterward?"

"Oh, there's lots of talk about afterward," Terk noted, "just nothing solid yet."

"Obviously, until this is done, there can't be any solid planning."

"Nope, there sure can't. And it's more complicated now

that a lot of partners are involved and …" Terk hesitated.

"What?" Brody asked curiously. "Surely there can't be more you haven't told me."

"Well, there is more," he admitted. "It's the first thing that I learned about after the accident that blew everybody up."

"Accident?" Brody asked in a dry tone.

"Well, let's just say, *attack*." Then Terk proceeded to tell Brody about the woman named Celia back in Texas.

"So they're attacking somebody in Texas, while we were all in France, getting attacked?" he cried out in astonishment. "And followed us here to England to continue to try to kill us?"

"Yes, but the real question is, how did they choose Celia? What do they know about Celia, and is she really carrying my child?"

"It's not like you to be uncertain."

"I'm not uncertain," he replied, "but, since I don't know this woman and obviously don't recognize her, … it puts me in a tough spot."

"Of course," Brody agreed quietly. "Maybe she went to a bank?"

Terk raised an eyebrow. "I've never donated," he said drily, "so that's out."

"Right, and when will you resolve all that?"

"When I'm sure that you guys are all safe and sound, without need for my support. At the moment, Celia is safe with Ice and Levi."

"Where's your brother in all this?"

"He's been helping us out steadily on the ground," Terk admitted. "We would have been lost without him. He's flying solo, seeing what he can find and turning up when we need him, plus being our intermediary to MI6. As you can imagine, we can trust few people when the chips are down like this." Terk shrugged. "It all comes down to family and close friends, anyone who is solid and has seen all the shit that can happen. They're far more than just a necessity when it comes to chaos like this."

"I understand," Brody murmured.

"Exactly. So, with Ice and Levi handling as much as they can on their end, and giving us a hand with data searches and working with Tasha and Sophia and Lorelei," he explained, "it's pretty insane. Sophia had been doing the odd contract with them and had traveled over with Merk to help out. She's paired with Wade now."

"Which is also pretty *un-fucking-believable.*" Brody shook his head and smirked nonetheless.

"I know, but so much is unbelievable right now that it seems to be the name of the game. It's all insane," Terk muttered.

Brody shifted his body again, checking to see just how bad every movement was. "Did you bring me clothes?" he asked.

"I think you need to stay here for a couple more days, now that you're awake," Terk replied. "It's too early for you to move much."

"Because, if you didn't bring me clothes"—he completely ignored everything Terk had just said—"it'll be a little embarrassing for everybody else as I walk out to the vehicle, but have no doubt that I'm going."

With that, another knock came at the door. The nurse stepped in, took one look at Brody, and sniffed. Turning to Terk, she stated, "Told you that he won't be an easy patient."

"No, he's not," Terk agreed, "and we really appreciate all that you've done for him so far."

"Well, *you* might, but he certainly doesn't."

At that Terk's lips twitched. "He isn't necessarily the best of patients. He does come from the heart, and we do need his particular brand of expertise."

"You can't take him away," she replied in alarm. "He's only just gotten out of the woods, and it'll take him weeks of therapy to get up and move."

Terk shot Brody a look. "You heard that, right?"

"You talk to her," Brody snapped, almost snarling at them. "You leave me to figure out what it'll take."

Terk shrugged. "You know you better than me. You can have a certain amount of assistance from me," he added, "but that's all I've got to give. I'll need to recharge as it is."

"Oh, you aren't kidding," Brody confirmed. "You've done nothing but give. You need all this to be over so you can get to Texas, before you'll ever really get recharged." Brody waved Terk and the nurse out of the room.

With them gone, he took a deep breath and tried to stand. Almost immediately his legs gave out, and he collapsed. Once again, back in his head, came that same voice.

I told you, she said cheerfully.

Well, instead of telling me, he growled, *why don't you help me?*

What is it you want me to do? she asked, and there was such curiosity but no judgment.

She had no idea how to help apparently. What kind of doctor was she? *I want to get up. I need to get dressed, and I want to get in the vehicle with Terk and go back to where my team is*, he explained. *Then I want to continuously heal going forward.*

Hmm, she muttered. *It might be possible, but it'll take some assistance.*

Yours to be exact, he demanded, sounding adamant.

Sure, she agreed. *Not certain it's in your best interests though.*

Maybe you don't get to make that decision, he growled.

Well, if you want my help, I should get some say in the matter, she stated matter-of-factly. *I won't return to back a losing horse.*

He stopped at that. *Do I look like a losing horse?* he raged.

If I don't assess this properly, it could go badly, and you'll go back down again. It took an awful lot to bring you to this point. I get that you're one of those big tough guys who figures, as soon as he's awake, he'd better be back to normal. But the fact is, you're not back to normal, she snapped and then continued. *And no amount of your deciding that you should be back to work will help.*

He growled in frustration.

She laughed. *I'll do an assessment, and, when I come back, we'll talk.* And, with that, she withdrew.

He cried out after her, *I don't know what kind of assessment you'll do, but you better make sure it's one that gives me the answers I want.*

But only silence came on the other end.

CLARY HEARD HIM and laughed.

Just something about these guys, who were so tough and so angry at their bodies for failing them, that she wanted to kick him in the shins to make him smarten up. But she'd also heard from her sister a lot about this team and about everything that was going wrong in their lives.

Clary genuinely wanted to help as much as she could, but, as her sister had said, Cara had made a lot of decisions to save Rick, and so she was worried about what would happen if she went so deep again with somebody else. Thus Cara declined to help Brody.

Not believing her, Clary dived in to help Brody, after she realized that he was out there lost and that her sister wasn't capable of reconnecting on the same level. But now? … Clary absolutely had to wonder if her sister was right after all. Clary had never seen it like this before. She was willing to do what was needed, and always had been, but it was a little on the bizarre side to see it play out in front of her like this.

Still, Clary was nothing if not curious, as she worked her way through Brody's system, checking to see how he was doing. She soon realized that he really had come a long way and, even now, was able to utilize her energy at an efficiency rate that she'd never seen before. Most of the patients she worked with didn't know how, whereas this whole team was amazing. Apparently they specialized in energy work, and it certainly made a difference from her perspective. It was incredible to see him healing and utilizing her energy, almost like an efficient machine, for his own needs.

The more she gave him, the more he grabbed, and at such a rate that she was in danger of running out, but for the abundance of the universe. Something to be said about understanding what was going on and what could be going on in his system.

When she came back out, he immediately asked, *Well?*

Wow, you don't even give a person a chance to adjust, do you?

No. What's the verdict?

You're burning through a ton of energy, she noted. *The good news is that you appear to understand how to utilize energy, and your body is using a lot of mine to make up for it.*

That's because Terk is running low, he said.

Terk has literally kept you alive, she stated bluntly, *completely by himself for at least three weeks, until Cara could send him some, and then I took over.* Clary huffed. *So I get that you want to run off and take your place as a key man on your team,* she murmured, *but there's an awful lot more to this than just you.* She felt his shock at her words.

Terk did that? Brody asked in an odd voice.

Yes, she confirmed. *My sister told me that, at one time, when all this happened, he was keeping all of you alive and protected.*

Jesus, can you imagine what that took out of him?

And I know he'd do it again. Thankfully, one by one, you've all come back. It's all due to his energy.

Yes. That's Terk. And he'd do anything for his team.

And he has, but it's also important that we don't pull more from him now than he can provide. He's also running his energy in ways that I've never seen anybody use before, as a defense system.

Yeah, that's Terk, and that's not all he can do, Brody stated. *But you're right, I can't keep draining him.*

Yes, I get that, and I agree, but you also can't be on your own just yet.

So, what's the workaround? he asked.

That's what I'm still trying to figure out.

No, he argued. *You've already figured it out. You just don't like the answer.*

She snorted. *Whoever gave you that kind of confidence?*

You'd be surprised, he snapped. *I can feel a hesitation on your part, but I don't know what the hesitation is.*

The hesitation is easy, she stated. *In order to do what you want to do, you'll need me.*

And the way she put it was so blunt, so clear, that he appeared stunned. *No*, he replied, *I don't think so.*

That's because you're not thinking, she muttered, *and that's a problem because you're reacting instead. And I get that, but, at the same time, we have a lot more to deal with here than just you.*

So, he said impatiently, *I'm not really somebody who likes to beat around the bush. You want to just tell me what the answer is then?*

The answer is, … I can help you, but … I need you to make a few commitments to me.

Like? he asked suspiciously.

She snorted at that. *Like, I need to make sure that you don't overdo it, and, when I say you're done, you allow me to knock it out.*

Knock what out?

My energy going to you obviously, she stated.

Hell no, he growled, riled and irritable.

Well then, you're not going anywhere. Then she disappeared.

Disconnected from his system, she sat here, thinking about it. She didn't want her sister put in any jeopardy either, and, where her sister was now in this entire mess would cause trouble. Her sister was out there in this world, physically with Terk's team, where everything was under attack, and that was concerning.

Very concerning, to be honest.

She would do anything to keep her sister alive. In fact,

it's one of the reasons they had developed their abilities as they had. She didn't know if Cara had said anything to the rest of the team or to Rick at this point in time, but it was because of her sister almost dying that both of them had gone under and learned how to do this. First, Clary had gone under, and her sister had come in afterward, trying to save her, doing everything she could to call Clary back home again. Yet, as soon as Clary started to recover and come back up, Cara had gone down from the effort of keeping Clary alive.

These were hard-learned lessons, but, once the twins had learned them, they had developed and expanded on those initial findings and kept on learning more. Now they did what Clary and Cara had thought nobody else in the world could even do. But apparently there was a whole team of people just like them.

Clary desperately wanted to be part of Terk's team. It was addictive having these kinds of abilities, but it was also lonely, and to know that others were out there who could do things like Clary could do was simply unbelievable. She needed to hold on to this group. She wanted to be a part of something bigger than a nine-to-five routine. But she also had to make sure that this Brody guy understood exactly what was required of her to keep monitoring his system.

If he wouldn't cooperate, well, … she wouldn't go there, at least for now. She heard him calling to her, but she kept ignoring him. Then she heard a desperate note to it. She popped back in. *Now what?*

Thank God, Brody said. *Look. Terk is leaving soon, and he says that, if he doesn't get the okay report from you, I can't go with him.*

Of course not. I won't do that, she stated in a quiet voice.

If nothing else, I am still a doctor, intent on healing you, not harming you.

He hesitated, *Please*, and she heard that plea from deep inside him.

The same conditions still apply, she noted calmly, *and, if you can't live with that, it doesn't matter what we're doing or what we have done so far to save your sorry ass because the answer will be a big and final no.*

Are you always this hard to get along with? he murmured.

Always, she declared, without a hint of remorse or hesitation, *and don't you ever forget it. While you're my patient, I'll do everything I can to keep you alive. Cross the line, and I'll take you down to where you can't do anything. If you can accept that, fine. Otherwise I am not giving in.* Then she concluded with finality, *We're done here.*

CHAPTER 2

C LARY LISTENED AS he cried out desperately, *What do you mean, we're done? Will you leave me?*

No, she stated. *You're my patient. Remember that part. But it means I'm not discussing this any further. I'll pop back in a couple hours. Do what needs to be done, and then I'll leave you to your world.*

You make it sound like my world is one that you don't want to visit, he murmured.

What I don't want to do is visit somebody who'll bitch and whine at me, while I'm trying to keep him alive, she clarified. *I'm here for a reason, and, if you can't live with it, I just won't talk to you about it. As soon as you are good to be out there on your own, I'll disconnect, and you can go on your merry way.*

Is it that easy? Because I don't think so …

It's never that easy, she said. *There's always a chance of something going wrong. There's always a chance of something else happening, but that's the least of my problems right now. Right now it's all about keeping your energy stabilized, and, as soon as you go into some kind of arrest*, she added, *I'll have to step in and make sure that I do what's needed to keep you alive.*

A long moment passed, before he murmured, *And you can do that so easily?*

Yes, I have done it several times already, … with you. She heard what felt more like a gasp. Speaking to him like this was also odd, but she was really enjoying it, and she was probably burning up too much energy in order to make it continuously happen, but she would examine that later when she got back out again.

All right, he replied quietly, *I'll trust your judgment.*

Well, that is more than I expected. That would be the first agreeable thing you've said so far. She laughed. *Honestly I don't think you trust anybody's judgment.* She was pushing all the right buttons.

I'm not very good at it, he admitted, *but, if you've kept me alive all this time, it would be selfish of me to cause trouble now.*

I suspect you do cause trouble about a lot of stuff in life, she said, *mostly because you care, but it's not okay. Because you care, it also makes you dangerous.*

Only to people who are in my way. Simply put, only people who are stopping me from helping those I care most about, he murmured.

Exactly, she replied. *So, my answer will still depend on whether you're capable of compromise.* She really needed him to understand the ramifications of his actions.

Are you sure? he asked. *Because your need to shut me down because you see some danger happening—overruling a decision of mine that would keep somebody else on the team alive—doesn't seem like a good compromise to me.*

Meaning?

You are a doctor, not fighting battles in the real world. So you won't necessarily understand what's happening if you're not close to me physically. Even then, you won't fully understand what we're going through and what is needed at the time. So, if you shut me down, it could very well put somebody else on my team in real danger.

And that will have to be a risk assessment I complete at the time, she noted calmly, or as calmly as she could. Because she understood in more ways than he did exactly what he was asking.

You also have to understand that my sister is with Rick and that I would do anything to keep her alive, she added passionately. *So there'll have to be a risk assessment on many levels, every time something happens. But you, … no offense intended,* and she made it very clear in her tone of voice, *are currently the weak link. And, if we need to snap my connection to you, I will. I'll keep you alive, but I can't have you putting other people in danger because you're not up for something.*

I understand. And, if I get weak out there, can you bolster my energy to get me home again?

Yes, depending on how bad it is.

Depending on how ugly things get, you mean?

Right, she said, with finality.

As with any plan, there are always these surprise parts and pieces that we must accommodate for, once the plan is in action, Brody explained.

There always are. There always will be, she murmured. *Again, we do the best we can in the moment, but there are no guarantees.*

Got it, he said. *Then please do what you can do to get me out of here, so I can go to where I need to be. Then hopefully we can come to an agreement with Terk and the rest of the team that keeps all of us alive.*

It's not just an agreement, she noted. *What they're doing? … They are planning an attack.*

Of course they are, he said a little desperately, *and I need to be part of it somehow. I need to see some closure to this nightmare.*

There is no closure for you right now, she stated, *and hon-*

estly, Brody, you're still in the baby stages. You are not doing anything or going anywhere in terms of a mission.

BRODY HATED IT, but she was right.

The team has already had weeks to recover and to assess. They have their defense planned and sorted out. They know the situation and understand what's going on, Clary explained in Brody's head. *You can't be a liability now, while they're all working hard to make this nightmare go away.*

He glared, wishing she were here in person to receive it. *I can help. I can do something to help my team.*

I don't see you here for the party.

"Shit," he yelled, facing the window. "That's Terk now."

Yes, he's leaving, Clary stated, *but that doesn't mean that he isn't coming back or that he hasn't made other arrangements.*

"But you also know," he stated out loud, an accusation in his tone, "that it's up to you to determine whether I get to leave or not, and … that just drives me nuts."

I get that, Clary noted, *and I know that there's one way we can make this happen. It's just more of a commitment than I was prepared to make.*

He looked around the room. "What is it?" he asked. "Why can't you show up here so we can talk face-to-face? … What can I do to make this happen?"

You being okay with my conditions. She glared at him. *And, … well, it can't happen right now,* she murmured to herself.

"That's not true," he cried out, holding his head. "Talk to me. Come on. It needs to happen now," he pleaded, as he watched Terk leave. "Don't you understand that he's leaving?"

Of course he is, she murmured. *He knows that it needs to happen.*

He frowned at the voice in his head. "Well, other things need to happen too," he snarled, "and I need to get out of here. With or without your help."

Let me think about it, and then we'll see. And, with that, she stepped out of his mind.

Brody was incensed that Clary could walk away so casually and so blasé, as if nothing he said would stop her.

He immediately looked around for clothes, anything more than the boxers he currently wore that would allow him to get out of here without drawing unwanted attention.

The nurse knocked and stepped into the room almost immediately. "Terk has left, but he said he'll call you in a few minutes."

He looked at her in surprise and then nodded hopefully. "Good. Can you find me my clothes?"

She glared at him. "Just because he'll call you doesn't mean that you get to leave."

"I need to leave," he snapped. "What'll it take to make somebody understand?"

"He said somebody else has the right to make that decision. It was *very* unlike Terk to say so, as he typically likes to be in control of the situation." The nurse looked at Brody and sniffed.

"Which I don't understand either," Brody confirmed, "because, as far as I'm concerned, no way anyone should decide but me. Terk also understands the scenario that we're facing, and, no matter what he says, he needs my help."

She shook her head. "You're still making progress, but you're not out of the woods," She noted his disapproving expression. "I'm not kidding. You'll find yourself in a very weakened state for a while, and you'll need a lot of therapy to get back on your feet."

Since he was already sitting upright on the bed, no point in jumping up and showing her that he could already do a lot. "I'm not as bad as you think I am," he replied.

She waved him away. "I've heard you yelling in here to someone, so I'll disagree with you there. I'll go get you a coffee. That'll help."

He just stared at her back, as she closed the door on him. How the hell would a cup of coffee help?

So much else was going on in his world right now that a cup of coffee sounded almost insulting. But basically it's what she could do, not necessarily what he could do.

And you have to be nice to other people, Clary snapped in his head.

"That is mandatory now?" he exasperated. "Am I not being nice?" he asked.

That nurse was hired to look after you. You have to let her do her job, without your emotional crap getting all over everything.

"I am," he snapped. "I'm not doing anything. It's just that … she doesn't understand that I'm already stronger than what she knows."

That's because she truly doesn't understand all your special gifts, so you have to accept that a lot of people don't believe you should be leaving.

"Of course," he muttered, "but my team will understand."

Well, Terk has left the decision up to me, Clary repeated.

Brody sat here with a fatalistic attitude, wondering how he would circumvent her decision because no way would she would let Brody leave. That was already a guarantee.

I will let you leave, she continued, making him bolt upright, *but, again, you have to agree to follow my terms.*

"Yes," he said instantly. He didn't know how he would live with it, but, if it meant getting out of here, he was all for it.

You're hardly in prison, she murmured.

"No, but I feel like a prisoner, and I don't want that. Not anymore."

I understand, she replied, *but sometimes you need somebody else to tell you to calm down and to stop pushing. And that'll be my job. So, if you can accept that, then fine. However, if you'll give me crap about it, it's a definite no. But be a good boy—*

"To get out of here and to get back to the compound, I'll be perfect," he murmured.

Well, take your time and let that sink in. I'll go talk to Terk. And, with that, she disappeared.

Brody couldn't believe his luck. He wasn't sure exactly what had changed in her attitude, but he was grateful for it. He just had to make sure she understood that she couldn't knock him down or stop him from doing something if he was in the middle of a mission.

That would be dangerous for everybody.

When his phone rang, he answered it, Terk laughing on the other end. Brody was immediately irritated.

"Well, I don't know how you managed to get her to agree," Terk noted, "but she is letting you move over to the compound. Still, I have also agreed to a couple stringent conditions, and, therefore, I'm sending somebody, probably a team, to come get you."

"A team?" he asked, uncertain. "Wouldn't stealth be better?"

"Oh, it's stealth all right," Terk stated. "I'm not sure you've ever seen this team before, and it will surprise you. It might even just be one guy on the front lines."

"Okay, … that sounds mysterious," Brody said. "Is it one of ours?"

"Nope," he murmured, a laughing tone in his voice, "but you have to remember that things are fluid right now."

"I don't care how damn fluid they are," Brody snapped, "just get me out of here. You have no idea what being lost out on the ethers was like."

"But I do," Terk corrected him, his voice hardening. "And you still have to behave yourself. We can't have you dropping off the grid, going rogue, and becoming a burden instead of an asset."

"I won't," he murmured. Brody was trying, and it showed in his voice.

"Well, you will do whatever you do because it's who you are," Terk admitted, "so I'm trusting Clary and her ability to keep you in line."

"Yeah, I'm not all that comfortable with that either. About her," he said cautiously, "can she really do what she says she can do?"

"First off, if you aren't comfortable with that, you aren't coming here. Second, not only is she an excellent empath and telepath, she's very adept at it. If you don't follow suit and if you intend to try to cheat your agreement with her, it won't go well for you," Terk murmured. "So I suggest you cage that beast within. You need to get along with everybody, especially her."

"Wow," he said. "How come we haven't had these people on our team if they're as good as you say?"

"I tried," Terk replied. "I tried to convince them at one point, but they really weren't interested," he murmured. "As you can see, they have abilities that go way beyond anything that we've ever seen."

"Well, that's what I mean. I'm surprised that they weren't part of the team because they sound so efficient at what they do. Almost too good to be true."

"They come with a huge price tag that means more than just money," Terk warned him.

Terk continued, and Terk's tone reminded Brody of his boss's op-voice, where he inherently warned them to not fuck this up.

"Sometimes I feel like they know more than they're necessarily willing to let on."

"Copy," Brody murmured. "I'm not ungrateful. Believe me. I just need to get to the next stage and to get back with everybody. I'll do my best not to be a burden, and I will try to heed your advice."

"And Clary's. Plus you'll find it strangely different now at headquarters. A lot of people are here."

"Of course. I understand. Terk, I belong there. I belong with the team," Brody stated. "Even if we relocate somewhere else, I still belong with the team."

"What if there is no team anymore?" Terk asked, his voice heavy.

"Then we'll make it work anyway," he declared. "Screw the government. We'll go independent."

At that, Terk burst out laughing. "You and the rest of them. It seems to me that you guys have it all worked out without me."

"That's what they're saying too, right?" Brody asked eagerly.

"Yeah, pretty much," Terk murmured, "but it's not that simple."

"It's not that difficult either," he reminded Terk. "We've done it before."

"Yes, but we've done it with government backing and with ample funding."

"True. But we've done more than that. We've relied on each other. It's huge that we had a ton of help and people working to lay out our path for us," Brody added, "but, if nobody else is around to help anymore, that's fine too. We will do *us* the way we always have."

"So you mean—"

"We won't require any of them or their funding," Brody stated.

"Well, we have their funding." Terk laughed. "I'm not even sure the government knows that, but I don't think it matters."

"Does it?"

"The money was supposed to be funding for our projects."

"I'm not sure what you're telling me, Terk."

"Before all this, we had a hefty sum come in to help with the operation of our team. I don't expect that anyone even knows or will be trying to take it away. And, since I moved it, they won't be able to locate it now."

"I'll think about all the problems that we've had in the past few jobs," Brody added, "but instinctively my mind says it was the government that did this."

"The problem with that is, we'll have one hell of an end game to flush them out and to make sure they can't do it again."

"I know." Then Brody asked, "Do you think your

brother and his team would help with that avenue?"

"Maybe, but we would have to convince them, and to spring it on them isn't fair. If there is no other way, then maybe, but they're in a difficult position. Their USA-based company will be in trouble, if they start dealing with our problems with the US government. We may get in the clear, but they will be on the government's radar."

"I know," Brody agreed. "I'll think about it some more."

"Well, you haven't got much time," Terk noted. "I've already sent a message to the nurse that you're being transported."

"That should make her happy." He snorted.

"She's not happy at all," Terk stated.

"Dang, I was supposed to get a cup of coffee out of the deal."

"Well, she's not even there anymore," Terk added, "and you have no clothes to leave, so take your time. I'm sending some your way but not a whole lot. Make do as you can and make sure you get on that transport safely." And, with that, Terk was gone.

Brody hopped up, a little wobbly still, looking around the room, trying to be as efficient as he could with his time and energy, but even searching for anything resulted in him sitting back down again, flushed and unsteady. Swearing at his weakness for cursing his life and for putting him in this position, he waited on the side of the bed for something to happen. For someone to come.

If the nurse was already gone, he wasn't sure of anything. When and how that had happened, he didn't know. What he did know was that he wasn't looking forward to asking for help.

And who the hell was coming to pick him up?

CHAPTER 3

C LARY SAT BESIDE Charles in the unmarked vehicle, staring at Brody's image projected from the apartment's internal cameras to this car's monitor. "He won't appreciate me being here."

"Doesn't matter whether he does or not." Charles looked directly at her. "According to Terk, it was part of your contract." He frowned. "Are you sure you want to get involved on the ground like this?"

"Not sure I have a choice," she admitted. "I'm already connected to him on a level that would be very difficult to disconnect from at this point. Besides, a sudden withdrawal like that could kill him."

Charles frowned and nodded stiffly. "I don't even try to understand all this, but I trust Ice and Levi. And, while I don't understand Terk either, I have worked with him many times. He is a man of honor, and, if he says this is necessary, then I'll do everything I can to make it happen."

She nodded at the older man, a man she had met only once. "He's kind of like … me," she murmured. "Unless you have the gift, you can't really fully understand, so it's better to just accept."

"Okay, but, when you do need something, you know you can call me." He looked over at her and patted her knee gently.

"Oh, believe me. I've been grateful each of the times I've had to call on your services."

"Presumably you'll still be available to us in the future?" he asked hesitantly.

She nodded. "If it's something I can do, I will be available."

"And that's always the trick, isn't it?" he asked.

She smiled sadly. "Just because we want to save everybody doesn't mean we can. And sometimes I have to say no because that is the only answer available."

"It's so sad when you do have to," he noted quietly.

"How is your granddaughter doing?" she asked.

He chuckled. "Oh, she's a pistol, that one." His affection was addicting at the moment. "She's still getting into trouble all the time, but now she at least has a partner to help her get back out of it."

Clary burst out laughing at that. "You know what? I'm not sure that's really what any parent or grandparent wants, but, in her case, I guess it's probably the best you'll get."

He nodded. "It absolutely is. The whole family is thrilled. They are a very good, a very well-suited match."

"Good," Clary said.

Just then their driver pulled up to an apartment building. It looked vaguely familiar, but she also knew it wasn't from her memories but from the energy.

"Do you think he's ready?" Charles asked her.

"He's ready," she said absentmindedly. "Nervous and excited, but definitely ready to be getting out."

"Makes it sound like he was in some sort of prison." Charles was confused.

"Well, he was in prison, sort of, and for a very long time," she replied.

"So I understand, not completely of course, except I have seen a lot of coma patients. Some people come out after a long time, saying that they heard and understood everything that happened to them. They were frustrated because they could never get anybody to understand that they were there."

She nodded. "And it's kind of like that, but, for Brody, it was different at times. Sometimes he was not even there, but he was conscious. I saw him traveling around. In his mind, he was a mess. Completely lost," she noted. "He's quite lucky to be alive."

He nodded, as he opened the car door. "You stay here, my dear. I'll be back in a minute."

She frowned and watched as he left. Something told her that she should go with him. She scrambled out of the vehicle, leaving the driver alone in the front seat and called out to Charles, "I'll come with you."

He looked surprised and shrugged. "Okay, I'm not sure why but okay."

"I need to," she murmured in a confused voice.

He frowned, yet nodded. "If you say so." And together they headed to the right floor and the designated apartment. He knocked on the outside door and noted how she shifted uneasily. "Something is bothering you."

"Yes," she confirmed, "and I'm not sure why, but time appears to be of an essence."

He again looked briefly puzzled. "We weren't followed."

"No, maybe not," she agreed, "but somebody has been here waiting."

He looked at her in concern, and she shrugged.

At the same time, the door opened, and there in front of them stood the man that she had worked so hard on, desperately trying her very best to keep him alive.

He looked at the two of them and asked, "Can I help you?"

"Yes," Charles replied gently. "I believe you're looking for a ride."

He looked at him suspiciously. "And do I know you?"

"Maybe not," he replied, "but you most certainly know an awful lot of my associates, particularly Levi, Ice, Terk, and Merk, … his brother."

Brody held up a hand. "Good enough. Terk just told me who you were."

"Let's go." Charles looked at him and held out a bag. "You'll cause less commotion if you change."

As he took the bag and started to head back inside, she reached out, grabbed his hand. "There's no time. We need to go. Now!"

Startled, Charles looked at her, but Brody didn't even hesitate. He stepped out with the bag still in his hand. "Let's go."

They raced back down to the driver, waiting, with the engine running, both of them half-supporting a weakened Brody. The driver looked up in surprise, as they got in. "That was fast."

"Drive. Drive out now!" she said urgently. "We have company."

He didn't need to be told twice, and he accelerated out of the parking lot, while Charles still stared at her, concern in his eyes. "That's a pretty handy little warning system you have, my dear."

"Maybe." She twisted to look behind them. "But this time, it's not telling me where the danger is coming from, and all I can say is that we're not out of danger yet."

"Good enough," Charles murmured.

As she watched and waited, the driver made a series of rapid turns, as if trying to dislodge somebody. She turned and looked at Brody. "Any chance that someone may have put a tracker on you? Think."

He stared at her in shock. "I have no idea. Can you see if there is one?" he asked hopefully.

At that, Charles looked from one to the other, but she reached around and checked the back of his neck and shoulders.

"I'm not seeing any injuries." She and Charles were working together now on either side of Brody, who was sandwiched between them.

"Me neither."

She then turned to ask Brody, "Any tenderness?"

He shook his head. "No."

"Good, maybe we'll be free and clear of this after all." And, just as she started to think what she was feeling might well be paranoia, the rear window exploded.

BRODY INSTINCTIVELY REACHED out and knocked her down, so that they were both flat on the seats. "You might have some inside line," he noted, "but I don't think you've ever seen much combat."

"Nope, I haven't," she admitted.

He wasn't even sure who she was. Nobody had identified themselves besides Charles. Yet, when she looked at his face, he had felt his heart beat faster. More like, he felt her, and, even then, he was quite unaware as to why.

He wasn't even sure who this ghostly Charles was, but

this woman? … He knew something about her.

With the mention of Terk working with the government, Brody could bet she was connected to MI6. With everything that had transpired already on French soil, now with his team on English soil, Terk's team probably could use all the help they could get, no matter where it came from.

Brody didn't want to say anything, but it was looking mighty fishy to have them tracked so easily. As they continued down on the road, he looked over at the driver. "Any signs of the shooter?"

"Nope, the vehicle behind us veered off." He had his radio out, talking to someone on the other end.

Brody was not privy to what was being said back. "So, just a warning then?"

"I'm not sure." His voice was beyond hard, with him looking out the back, he looked almost murderous. "I've called for help, but we'll keep going in the same direction."

"Doesn't that just mean that somebody else will come and unceremoniously shoot us?" the woman cried out from the bowels of the seat.

"I hope not," Charles said.

"Getting shot was really not on today's agenda," Brody stated in such a prosaic way that Charles burst out laughing.

"Love the attitude," he said warmly. Charles smiled at him benignly. "When you are my age," he noted, "you, too, will have seen everything."

"This shouldn't have been a surprise," the driver added, also in on the conversation.

Charles added, "I wasn't thinking that they had Brody's location locked down."

They were all on the same page, except for Brody. "I

should have listened to Terk. He was right," Brody admitted.

"Well, if he says something to you in the future, listen," the driver said, frustrated.

"Generally Terk is right. It's kind of scary too," the woman murmured.

"You know Terk?" Brody asked her.

"I do," she stated, looking at Brody oddly. Then she chuckled. "You really don't know who I am, do you?"

"No, I don't," he replied, quietly studying her. "You arrived with Charles, so I figured you were with him."

"Ah. Not quite, am I, Charles?"

"No." He laughed, then smiled. "Not quite."

"Well, I'm glad you all have some kind of game going on to keep me guessing," Brody snapped, "but presumably, if I don't know, it's not important."

"No, maybe not," she said, one eyebrow arching as if surprised at his attitude.

He shrugged. "I've got way too much going on in my world right now, so best to let it go. Anyway it's nice to meet you, whoever you are."

Just then the vehicle took a series of sudden shifts, and they pulled in tight into a garage.

Brody turned and looked around. "Is this the compound?"

"No, not yet," the driver murmured, "but we have more company, so this place is what we need right now."

"Crap," Brody said. "Do you have any weapons on board?"

"I do," he confirmed, "but you're not authorized to use them."

He looked over at Charles. "Seriously?"

Charles smiled and handed over a pistol. "That's all I've

got for you, young man." He winked at Brody, as if he knew him. "I believe you know how to use it."

"Absolutely," he stated. He looked around. "Now, will we go chase this down?"

"I don't know," the driver replied. "I don't want to leave Charles."

"In that case," Brody said, "I'll go. You can both cover me."

And, with that, he slipped out and took off.

CHAPTER 4

CLARY WATCHED AS Brody disappeared, realizing that he really didn't know who she was. It was kind of an odd letdown. She'd been in his mind, and he had been in her sight for so long that he felt like a part of her—and she a part of him. After all that, to find out that he had absolutely no clue was a disappointment in so many ways.

At the same time, it made sense. Of course he didn't know who she was. It just seemed, well, … odd. Regardless, she watched as he swept to the other side of the car. She murmured to Charles, "Is it safe for him to go alone?"

"No," he replied. "There are definitely some safety factors here, but we can't mitigate the threat if we have somebody following us like this. Much better that we figure out who they are and take them out. So, we need to give them a target."

"Nice and yet terrible," she noted.

He chuckled. "Remember, my dear. This is the kind of life that they live."

"Maybe," she said. "It's not what I'm used to though."

"Of course not, and I sympathize because it's quite an eye-opener to find yourself in a situation like this. It can mess with your mind."

She watched as Brody disappeared through a door. "Where's he going? Do you know?" She twisted around, but, with the back window blown out, she had a perfect view, and then it dawned on her that they were sitting ducks, out in the open like this. She fed Brody a little more energy. He'd been weaker originally but was gaining strength. "Won't we do anything about that window? We'll stick out like a sore thumb."

"We have another vehicle coming," the driver explained.

"Ah, good," she said. "That will help."

"Indeed." He smiled in her direction. "You can just settle back and relax."

She wasn't so sure that was on the docket, but she understood his offering. And she was more than happy to accept, but for the fact that she was waiting for a very sick man to get his ass back into the vehicle.

She was feeding him as much energy as she safely could, being careful that he didn't get into a euphoric high with it or do anything stupid.

When he came back, he looked around at them and explained calmly, "Nobody out on the street. Whoever fired the shot has disappeared. Also, I don't see anyone around paying us any attention."

"Good," the driver said, as he turned and looked at Charles and Clary. "The other vehicle is here now, so we can switch safely."

The garage door next to them buzzed. Every garage was connected to another, so they didn't have to exit the same way they had entered. Clary pondered that, as their driver entered the newly accessible garage. "This is pretty convenient, isn't it?" she murmured.

Charles beamed at her. "Convenience is big in our world."

She laughed. "Not just convenience, secrecy too."

"Absolutely." Charles smiled brightly at her. "You're doing really well at catching up."

At that, Brody gave her an odd look, but she just smiled at him and didn't say anything.

Then something dawned on his face and recognition hit him. "It's you. The voice in my head."

"Yeah, and you took your own sweet time figuring it out." She wouldn't let him live it down, and he seemed to understand perfectly. Still it was hardly the time to talk. And, with that, they transferred into a government-issued smoky-windowed vehicle.

Once they were safely settled in their current vehicle, leaving their other vehicle to be picked up by Charles's team, their driver drove out of the garage and headed out again. She asked, "How much farther do we have to go?"

"It's a bit of a ride yet," the driver replied.

"Okay," she said in surprise. She frowned at that. "Do you think they know where we're going?"

"They might," the driver replied, "but then they don't really have any reason to follow us at this point. They've already blown that chance." She wasn't so sure about that, but she was willing to give them a chance to see what they could figure out. And, sure enough, by the time they were closer to their destination, she was feeling pretty perky, satisfied that they were out of danger.

That alarmed feeling at the back of her mind was receding.

The men continuously looked around and didn't have the same sense of satisfaction that she did. Though they did seem to relax the farther they drove.

She looked over at Charles. "I guess technically you may not be allowed to operate with Terk's team. Do you feel you can?"

He shook his head. "Nope, not technically, but we don't always check in as closely as we should when it comes to some of our government restrictions. We do what is necessary for our friends."

She smiled and settled back, waiting for the journey to come to an end.

BRODY, EVER ALERT, watched as they pulled into a huge commercial-looking area and were let into what appeared to be a secure garage, very quickly. Brody looked around and frowned. "Not exactly the most appealing."

"Nope, but they've done a lot of rapid modifications," Charles got out and quickly opened up the car door for the woman. He clearly had a soft spot for this one, and it showed in every interaction. "I leave you here, my dear."

She stepped out and gave him the gentlest of hugs and a kiss on the cheek. With a hint of sadness, it was obvious how much she appreciated him. "Thank you." Her voice was soft, almost feathery. And, with that, she looked at Brody expectantly. "Are you ready?"

Frowning, he was lost in thought, yet her words pulled him back. "I didn't realize you were coming along," Brody replied curiously.

"Yeah." She smiled. "I thought for sure that you would have figured that out by now."

He stared at her, but, at that point, they were saying goodbye to the rest of the group. As the driver and Charles drove away, Brody turned to face her. He really needed some answers. "Do you want to explain that comment?"

Then a side door opened, interrupting him yet again. Out came a woman, very similar in facial expressions and demeanor as the one who had been the bane of Brody's sanity, ever since he had come out of the coma.

The newcomer's face lit up. "Clary." She raced forward, throwing her arms around the other woman. She laughed and held her sister close.

Despite his initial interactions with Clary, this looked like a functional family.

Then the woman walked over to Brody and introduced herself. "I'm Cara, Clary's sister. We're twins."

At that, he turned to Clary, all his suspicions coming to haunt him.

Clary murmured, "We were originally triplets but our brother died." With Brody's gaze deadlocked on her, she just shrugged. "The only way I can keep you safe is if I am close by."

"So, nice attempt to throw me off by speaking to me telepathically, making me think you wouldn't be here."

"I wasn't trying to throw off anything, or anyone for that matter," she protested.

"I had no idea that you were coming."

"Well, it's the best answer." Her expression was almost maddening. She turned back to her sister, as if she'd had enough of this conversation with Brody. "You are looking divine," she whispered, studying her sister.

Cara just laughed. "Trust you to say something like that." She continued her survey of Clary with a critical eye. "You, on the other hand, look a little worse for wear. A bit worn out."

"Yeah, we were attacked and shot at on the way over." She wrinkled her face up into an odd look. "I can't say it was the highlight of my life."

"Right. Welcome to the club," Cara replied, worry in her voice, yet trying so hard to lighten the mood. "Even though we walk with one foot on each side, it's still odd to see how often this group puts themselves in danger."

Clary turned back to Brody and looked at him. "Are you coming?"

His feet moved automatically, but Brody had absolutely no idea what to say. This woman was not who he expected and looked nothing like what he thought she would look like. Here she was, this absolutely stunning blonde, who he'd thought was working with Charles or was maybe even a family member. Now he knew why he'd felt so drawn to her when they met.

Yet it made no sense, but to find out that she was the woman who had kept him alive this whole time had changed his perspective. The experience turned out to be … eye-opening.

He stepped forward into the compound, and immediately the rest of the group was on him, everybody pulling him in for a hug. To him, it felt like he was engulfed in a sea of arms. He laughed, as he realized that all his team, everybody he loved, was here waiting for him.

It took a few moments for everybody to calm down, but the chattering kept on, as everybody was busy introducing him to the women he didn't know, and he got a chance to greet the others that he did know but hadn't seen in a long time.

When Tasha got a hold of him, she just wouldn't let go. Brody held on tight and whispered, "So glad you're okay."

She pulled back, looked up at him teary-eyed, and murmured, "And you." She was trying to find the right words, but there was no easy way. "That was one of the worst times of my life. And to know that you were almost lost to us for … so long." She shook her head, and he saw her tears.

He reached out with a thumb and gently wiped them away. "I'm fine now," he murmured.

She grinned. "Well, not quite fine, at least not according to Terk and Clary."

"So you know about Clary too?"

"Nope, … we only just found out about her from Terk," she stated, the hurt evident in her voice. "But anybody who can keep you safe and everybody else on this team alive," she added, clearly savoring the idea, "believe me. We're all going to love her."

Brody smiled. "She has certainly done a hell of a job on me. I felt like I was in never-ending darkness and in never-ending pain. I was the lost soul with nobody to talk to, nobody to cry out to and to ask for help." He shuddered under the weight of that realization and the remembrance. "Not a scenario I ever want to be put in or to feel ever again."

She reached up, hugged him close once more, and affectionately stroked his cheek. "No, not anything we ever want." She walked him over to Sophia, someone he'd already been introduced him to earlier, but still it seemed that Tasha wanted Brody to feel comfortable and to get familiar with the new faces. "This is Sophia. She worked for Terk's brother's team before she came to be with us."

Sophia stood and shook hands with him. "I'm really happy to hear that you'll be okay. Everybody here has been terribly worried about you."

He smiled. "And I appreciate the worry, but honestly I'm feeling much better."

"You might be feeling much better," Gage walked closer, "but we all know just how rough that trip out of a coma was."

Brody looked at his buddy. "You too?"

Gage nodded. "All of us to some degree. Damon got off the best. Well, scratch that. Terk maybe, and then Damon. While the rest of us all? … We've all been brought out one at a time, as we came out of the terrible dark place."

"Man, I never thought I would be slow in something. It's as if I have forgotten about progress. It was awful," Brody admitted.

"You almost died," Clary said quietly at his side. "You get to cut yourself some slack for that."

"Almost?" he asked, with a lopsided grin.

She smiled. "Yes. I know you don't believe it, and I get that, but you have no idea just how far from coming back you were."

"And I owe that return journey to you, right?" He still wasn't sure how all that worked, but he was also aware of all the people looking at him. He didn't even really know how to react to Clary. It's like he had just found out something amazing and important in life, and he would have an audience while he tried to adjust to the news.

Cara walked closer and whispered, "You were basically gone."

As if a cord had been yanked, he was plucked back to reality.

"So, if you remember any of your energy-working lessons," Cara murmured, "you know how close you came to not coming back."

He looked at her in surprise, and she nodded, like she was asking him to get that through his thick head.

"We're not kidding. It was a tough, … tough scenario for quite a while."

Brody nodded slowly. "Then I thank you," he murmured to Cara. "I hadn't realized how bad it was."

"Our patients never do." She smiled. "We always try to keep things calm and to assure you that it isn't so bad, but, in your case, it was definitely bad."

He nodded slowly. "And it was really you and your sister?"

"Mostly my sister," Cara admitted. "I ended up quite busy with everything here, and I knew my sister had the ability to, well, … let me just say that, if you'd died, there is a chance that she would have been there, waiting to kick your ass back onto this side."

That's impossible. It had to be. Maybe? … He stared at Cara in shock.

Cara nodded with renewed vigor. "So play nice. Clary really did save your life."

CHAPTER 5

I T TOOK THEM a solid hour to be assigned rooms and to get sorted. Then Clary handed the bag Charles had brought to Brody. "It's only a couple changes of clothes. We'll have to arrange to get you more."

He nodded almost numbly and took the bag. "I never did say *thank you.*"

She looked at him in surprise, then almost laughed. "See? That wasn't so hard. Now go on ..." She waved him toward the bed. "You need to rest. ... Doctor's orders."

"That's hardly paramount today."

"And yet it feels like it should be," she noted.

"I feel like an ass, for some reason."

"We'll talk later," she said. "What you need right now is rest." He frowned at that. Her expression changed, compartmentalizing Brody's energy from Brody's beast that Cara had warned her about.

"Will you always be ordering me around?"

Her shell broke somewhat to reveal a half smirk. "Maybe. Will you always need to order me around?"

And, for the first time since he resurfaced, he grinned. "Maybe." Then he headed into his room without a backward glance.

She closed the door firmly behind him, yet still he heard her calling out, "I'll be in to check on you a bit later." Once again she had to remind Brody that she was a doctor, with superpowers, and he was in her care.

Yet he was arguing—mostly with himself—and telepathically.

How the hell had that happened? I have no clue how Clary ended up in charge of me, but, … if there was anybody in this world who would ensure I was still alive and doing okay, it would be Clary. And what's with that sense of wonderment— when I first met her and didn't know who she was? Why is it still with me?

Clary walked into the room she'd been assigned and fell onto the bed, her shoes still on. She was exhausted in many ways. When the door opened without a knock or any warning, she smiled and called out, "I sure hope you brought a coffee with you."

"Will you sleep if you get coffee?" Cara asked worriedly, then sat down on the bed beside her. "You look like shit."

"Yeah. And thanks for that by the way," she quipped. "I'm just tired. It took quite a bit to keep him going long enough to get us here in one piece. He thinks he's a lot stronger than he is, so it's taking a lot out of me."

"And yet you let him come."

"Yeah." She opened her eyes to look at the sister she adored. "It also gave me a chance to come to you."

At that, her sister wrapped her up close. She was worried about her. "I hope it was the right decision," Cara noted.

"Is it that dangerous here right now?" Clary asked.

"It's like, … at times it's just too much. It seriously is. Like bad news all around."

"Well, in that case, we'll have to figure it out fast," Clary stated, "because Brody was dying to get here. That's the problem though. He could be dying." She was deep in touch with Brody and drifted a bit, until Cara held her tightly. Clary nodded, addressed her sister. "We won't do much about it. I know he only realized who I was when we got out here at the compound. So he's still in a bit of shock and in a state of denial."

Her sister stared at her, and then, in a few moments, she started to laugh. "Oh my," Cara said, "I hadn't expected that."

"I know, right? Honestly I didn't either. I thought the same connection I feel with him, he would feel with me."

At that, her sister stared at her in worry. "Is it … Is it deep?"

"Of course it is," Clary confirmed, "and you knew it would be."

"Well, I knew it could be troublesome," Cara protested, "but I was hoping you'd distance yourself and not get too involved."

"Well, I failed. Somewhere along the line, it seemed more important to get him back than it was to keep myself separate. And, since I was fighting for his life, I realized that I had to let go of some of that detachment, which I so desperately needed."

"Oh Lord," Cara whispered sadly. "In other words, you're as hooked as I am. I'm sorry. That wasn't my intent."

"I am hooked, but I'm not sure that it will have as positive of an outcome as you have experienced."

"We have to keep the faith on that," Cara replied.

"Yeah, well, you and I both know how hard this job can be."

"Sometimes I do wonder why we do this." She focused on her sister, a worried expression on her face.

"Because we really have no choice," Clary murmured.

"This is who we are, so, in order to be true to who we are, this is where we have to be." And there was so much truth to her words that it brought tears to both sisters' eyes.

"Well, I really hope this works out for you," Cara said. "Otherwise I'll hate myself forever for having dragged you into it."

At that, Clary looked at her and laughed. "Like that'll work," she teased, trying to make Cara feel better.

Cara stared at her affectionately. "You and I both know that we have a tendency to do what we feel we need to do."

Clary added, "And we jump right in regardless."

"I know," Cara admitted, "but I don't want you hurt."

"We get hurt with every job," Clary stated. "We lose a little bit of ourselves, while we save someone else. It's just part of the price of what we do."

"Still, I was hoping"—Cara paused—"that maybe this time would be different."

"Well, guess what?" Clary laughed. "It isn't."

At that, her sister leaned over, gave her yet another hug. "Do you want a hot shower? I have clothes here, so maybe that will help."

"I would love some clothes," Clary replied. "I did bring a bag, but I didn't bring much, not knowing how long I would be here."

"Yeah, and that's looking like it'll be a lot longer than you thought, right?"

"Isn't it always?" she said sarcastically. "You would think we'd have learned our lesson by now. The problem is, we've never been exiled before. We've never had to hide like this, so all of our normal ways of operating had to be stopped in order to make this workable, and that means no shopping, no ordering online, and just making do. You seem to be doing okay with it though, don't you?" Clary asked.

"I am okay with it," Cara replied, "for now at least. There have been lots of ups and downs, but, as long as I have Rick beside me, then it's all good."

"I'm so happy for you. Rick looks like a very nice man."

"He is, but then you don't need me to say that. You can see that energy all for yourself."

She grinned. "Yeah, I can. I'm just not sure how I'll handle Brody."

"According to everybody else around here, Brody is the man." Cara grinned.

"We'll have to see about that. Maybe this time both of us will get lucky."

"We haven't been very lucky in love so far," Cara admitted.

Clary nodded. "If anything, it's been the worst for both of us."

"I know," Cara agreed, "but not everybody can understand the kind of work we do."

"These guys at least should manage that much," Clary noted.

"You'd think," Cara added in a dry tone. "I am so confused. We've kept them alive and brought them back from the brink of death. You would think that they're supposed to be okay with it, but we know how that goes."

"That's not always the case with everyone," Clary said.

"No, but these are two young men, both healthy, both happy, and now with a connection to us that we never expected," Cara stated, "so let's give them the benefit of the doubt and see how it works out."

"And this is you saying that too," Clary noted in amazement.

Cara grinned. "That's because I'm in love," she whispered, "and it's pretty damn fine. How about the same thing for you?"

"Well, we certainly have that bond," Clary confirmed, "and I've felt your emotions the whole time, but that doesn't mean I'll have the same result in my case."

"Well, we'll see," Cara replied. "We aren't twins for nothing. I can feel your interest. I can feel your connection to him, and I can feel his connection to you. He has no clue what to do with any of this, but he's definitely interested." Cara grinned at her sister.

"Good," Clary said, "because so am I."

IT WAS HARD to imagine feeling more like an idiot than Brody already did, once he realized that the woman who had traveled from the apartment and ended up with him here was Clary. The same woman who had been in his head and who supposedly had control over him in a way that he'd never experienced before.

He felt a combination of resentment, embarrassment, and joy because there had been that connection, that sense of something special about her. Now he understood more; yet it just made him wary. He'd never been up against something like this before, and he wasn't sure how to handle it.

The fact that she was completely nonchalant and relaxed about it all didn't help. She was also very close to her twin sister. The two of them were definitely not identical but similar enough in looks that he also felt a kinship with Cara.

How the hell did that work?

Brody shook his head, left his room, and joined his team

in the main room. Brody looked over at Rick, sitting at a computer, pounding away on something and getting frustrated. Nobody would let him do anything either. At this point, nobody was letting Brody get close to anything important, and it was driving him nuts too. He dropped in the nearest chair with a grunt.

When Clary sat down beside him, she said, "You'll need to calm down that energy."

"Or what?" he snapped, glaring at her.

She raised an eyebrow. "Or you'll burn up too much energy, and the healing that could be happening won't get done."

He mainly felt shitty because it wasn't her fault. She'd done a lot to keep him alive, and he was being an ungrateful bastard. At the same time just knowing that he was an ungrateful bastard didn't help. He groaned softly. "Sorry, I'm not trying to be a bear," he explained. "It's just frustrating that they won't let me do anything."

"Because you're obviously still not ready to do anything," she murmured. "I get that you're frustrated. You're stressed, and you want to be back to the way you were, but you're just not there yet."

"When will I get there?" He glared at her.

"Not anytime soon at this rate," she murmured.

Nobody has ever been okay with someone telling them they are basically useless. He immediately got up and walked over to the coffeepot to pour himself a cup. She didn't say anything, which was good, because he wasn't sure that he could trust what would come out of his mouth.

She stood beside him now. "Are you sure there isn't something you can do that would be less demanding?" she murmured.

"Like what?" He raised his empty hand in frustration. "If there was something I could do, and I knew what it was, I'd be doing it."

"Are they keeping you out of it intentionally?"

"I think they are, but I'm not sure. They may just not have taken the time or energy to let me in on their plans. There is a slim chance of that." He had no idea where this sudden urge to clarify himself was coming from.

She nodded. "That makes more sense. I know that they're short on manpower and that they're struggling with whatever the scenario is," she murmured. "I would imagine it's more a case of not knowing how to make good use of you because they also don't know where your abilities currently are and how you can contribute right now."

"Well, having you around as a babysitter won't give them any confidence in me." He struck a nerve, and she stared at him with such a flat gaze that he immediately felt shitty again. "You have the ability," he said, "to make me feel like I'm a terrible person."

She burst out laughing. "Oh no. *That* …" she stated succinctly, "is not my ability but yours."

She was concerned, yet the banter was not helping at all, in Brody's opinion.

"If you want to be treated like a child," she murmured, "then act like a child. If you want to be treated like an important part of the team, then act like that." And, with that, she turned and walked over to sit beside her sister, who was helping Mariana with the supply list.

He wondered at her words, unsure of what to do, as he pondered it. He didn't get much chance because, all of a sudden, Terk was here, frowning at Brody, which he could use less of right about now. "I'm fine, you know."

Terk nodded. "I do know. Cara and Clary have given me regular updates."

"Where did you find them?" Brody stared at his friend, as Terk led them both to an empty desk nearby, where they both sat down with their coffee. "I mean, they're both rather incredible," Brody acknowledged.

"They are," Terk confirmed. "I tried very hard to get them to join the team, but they didn't want anything quite so restrictive."

"I guess that's fair," Brody murmured. "I'm just grateful that they decided to help out now."

"Me too," Terk said quietly, "and I think it was also the right time in their lives."

"In what way?"

"They lost both of their parents recently. Cara was dealing with a difficult patient scenario and needed a break. Unfortunately for her, the break she got was another difficult case," Terk added, with half a smile. "But she's been really good for a long haul now."

"And she saved Rick's life too?"

"Yes, absolutely. Just as Clary has done for you."

Brody shook his head at that. "I still don't even understand what they did. Yet they've obviously done something because I'm here and not lost in the ethers. I do wonder about that period, as I'm coming up short on the recalls. I do feel I would have made it out on my own." He sent Terk a sideways glance. "Eventually."

"And you might have," Terk noted calmly, "but it could have taken you a decade."

Brody sucked in his breath at that. "Well, that put things into perspective."

"It depends on whether you want to live the next ten

years or to just float. We've seen both cases, when someone goes through such a difficult time."

"I guess," Brody murmured. "That wasn't exactly the answer I thought I would get from you though."

"If you don't have a connection to Clary, that's fine," he said. "I'm not trying to force this relationship on anybody, but I will expect that, while she's here doing her job, you will listen to her."

Just enough firmness filled Terk's voice to make Brody realize that Clary had probably said something to Terk.

"What I can't have," Brody explained, "is her shutting me down when we're in the middle of something."

"I agree with that in part," Terk murmured, "and I saw it happen with Cara and Rick. They worked it out, and I expect you will do the same with Clary."

"Maybe I can't. Maybe I'm not able to work it out. Maybe—"

"Are you saying you can't, or are you asking me to assure you that you can?"

"I don't know," he admitted.

"Listen, Brody. You can be difficult at the best of times, and you also have a tendency to go headfirst into danger. Just know that she's trying to avoid your going so far ahead that you put yourself into *mortal* danger, where even she can't bring you back. You know that we are all a ticking time bomb, and we all can take ourselves out."

"Well, I'd like to avoid that too," Brody agreed. "It just seems so odd that she would have that kind of intimate knowledge. I can't …"

"What are you saying?"

"I don't like anybody having power over me."

"She doesn't. She's a doctor, and she is necessary for

your recovery." Terk frowned. "Brody, I'm not sure how to make you see reason on this point."

"This is too much, Terk," Brody added.

"That's why Cara and Rick had to find a middle ground. I expect you to find it in your own time, within your own rights as well."

Brody pondered that, as Terk sat here comfortably, drinking coffee. "How come there's nothing here I can do?"

"You tell me if there's anything you can do," Terk replied immediately. "We need all hands on deck."

"So why am I being shut out then?" Brody asked in frustration.

"Are you being shut out?" Terk asked. "Or have you shut yourself out? Or maybe you haven't let yourself in."

"What does all that doublespeak mean? You sound like Clary now," Brody cried out in frustration.

Several others turned to look at them and then went back to work.

"It means," Terk replied, "that you haven't actively rejoined the team. And, until that happens, they'll let you heal and do your own thing, with the assumption that, at some point in time, you'll feel good enough to jump in."

"Oh, damn," Brody muttered. "I wasn't thinking of it like that."

"That's because you're still thinking that you're on the outside and injured, and that's what you're projecting. So that's what they're perceiving. You need to let go, Brody."

"Shit," he muttered to himself. "Why the hell does it always feel like I'm the bad guy?"

At that, Terk burst out laughing. "I don't think there are any bad guys on our team." He chuckled. "Listen. I understand your frustration. I understand that sense of wondering what the hell happened and why you're not at the forefront of everything."

"But—"

"No buts. When you're ready, and when you see a need or something that you can do, I expect you'll jump right in," Terk explained, still smiling. "However, a word of warning. Until that happens, please take as much time as you need to feel like you're back to normal and can do something." With that, he stood. "Now I've got to go. The women have a shopping list for me."

"Let me come too," Brody said. Terk turned and frowned at him. Brody shook his head. "That's hardly a good use of your time, Terk," Brody replied sharply.

"What is?" Terk asked.

"Sitting in a vehicle and doing nothing?" Brody scoffed.

"Well, I would be doing something," Terk corrected him, "and, whether you like it or not, there is still an awful lot going on out there that we aren't necessarily happy with."

"All the more reason for me to come. I'll be a pair of eyes but not a whole lot else," Brody murmured.

CHAPTER 6

J UST THEN CLARY, seeing the intensity of the conversation and sensing the change in Brody's physiology, walked over and sat beside the two of them. "What's going on?" she asked. Terk raised an eyebrow, and she shrugged. "His blood pressure is up. His pulse is racing, and I'm just trying to figure out what's happening."

"It's all good," Brody said immediately.

She looked over at him, and her lips twitched. "You know what? I really won't just shut you down if nothing is happening. You know that, right?"

"I *don't* know that." He frowned at her. "I'm still trying to adjust to the fact that I'm not in control."

"And, when you are in control, you'll know it," she replied, a bit annoyed at his attitude. She turned back to Terk. "So what's happening?"

"He wants to come shopping with me."

Her eyes widened in astonishment. "Shopping?"

Brody glared. "Yes, but you don't have to make it sound quite so bad. I just wanted to do something."

She thought about it and nodded. "I can see that." She looked at Terk. "What do you think?"

"I don't know." Terk shrugged. "I think there's a lot to be said for it, but, at the same time, I'm not sure he's ready."

"On the other hand, he's not likely to get ready if he

doesn't get out and get around. He needs to manage on his own and to get his senses back," she noted calmly. "He's still not operating on those at 100 percent," she told Terk.

"Just out of curiosity," Brody said, leaning forward, "what would you estimate I'm operating at?"

"Your senses? I'd say about 60 percent," she replied immediately.

He stared at her in shock. "I would have said a lot higher."

"Of course because you're thinking what you feel is the actual fact of what's going on in your system. Sorry to burst your bubble, but it's not," she stated. "You're not there yet, which is also why going shopping would potentially be a good way to exercise some of those senses again and to see if we can get them moving in the right direction." She looked at Terk, then shrugged. "I'd agree with the shopping idea."

Brody growled. "I know I should be grateful, but it pisses me off that somebody—you—had to even acknowledge what was good and what wasn't good about going *shopping*."

She turned and looked at him. "Unless, of course, you want to stay here and go to bed."

He opened his mouth, then snapped it closed, finally adding, "I'm going shopping."

She just smirked and walked away.

"DOES THAT MEAN she's not coming with us then?" Brody asked Terk.

"If she's not coming, she doesn't think there's any need to."

"Good," Brody muttered. "It's really weird being tethered to her. It's …"

"I'm sure it's weird for her too," Terk noted.

"I don't know. I think she's more used to it than I am."

"Probably because she has done this many times over with multiple patients."

Brody went silent.

Terk nodded. "She's had patients she's lost, and some she hasn't. There's always a cost to her. So, before you get on your high horse and get angry again, you might remember that she's taken a lot of time and energy for this assignment and invested a lot of herself in you."

"I know that," Brody said. "I really do, and it's frustrating because I have to be reminded of it."

"It didn't have to be that way, but it's not a bad idea to keep some things in focus."

Brody groaned. "Got it. It'll just take a bit."

"Of course it will," Terk agreed. "If you're up for it, let's go for a ride. You can help me pack all this stuff into the vehicle. It's unbelievable how much these ladies require on a regular basis."

Brody laughed. "I hardly think it's the ladies who require it all. I'm sure it's the fact that you're feeding … how many of us now?"

"About fourteen, maybe sixteen now, or just a second." He seemed to be mentally counting in his head. "It's sixteen—sixteen for sure."

"Pretty amazing."

"It is, but it's also a lot of supplies."

"Are we okay for money?"

Terk snorted. "We are for the moment."

Brody was excited that he would get to do something, though a little worried he may have bitten off more than he could chew, when he got to his feet and immediately felt wobbly.

"Let me go see if they've got the list ready." At that, Terk walked over to the ladies and accepted the list. He looked at it for a moment, then nodded and walked away to join Brody. "You ready? Let's go." And, with that, he headed toward the rear door. "We're this way," he said.

"Good. Anything you want to fill me in on?" Brody asked. "Like why we're doing all of this so cloak-and-dagger? I still think it'd be a good idea to lead our attackers right in. We could deal with it and be done."

"If it were that easy, it would be fine," Terk replied, "but just one fatality out of this group is not acceptable. Any more loss of life would splinter us in ways you can't imagine."

As Brody looked around, he realized the impact of everybody partnering up, and how many would be horribly affected at the loss of just even one member. He had to agree. "I'm so not used to considering these other members added to our group," he admitted. "It's not just us, but it's like Calum has his own team, with Mariana and the little guy. Gage and Lorelei, Wade and Sophia, and so on."

"That's one way to look at it," Terk noted. "The other way is that we're just one big team. No way that a loss will be acceptable. We lost two admins already. That's enough. Now, we're coming back stronger than ever, and there's absolutely no need for anybody to go down again."

"That's heartwarming but hardly practical out in the world," Brody said quietly. "The compound is good though."

"Yeah, it's a good place. It needs to be," Terk stated. "We need people in a position to do what we need them to do. That'll be tough for a little bit. Once we get clear of this continued attack on us, then it won't be too bad. But we're not there yet."

"No, we're not," Brody admitted, "but, with you at the helm, I am sure we'll get there."

Terk looked at him in surprise. "I wouldn't let me off the hook so easily," he warned. "I should have seen this coming."

"You've always said you weren't infallible," he replied. "And that you could only get information that showed itself. This is a case in point, I guess."

"So what's the point of having our gifts then," Terk murmured, "if I can't see the danger to ourselves?"

"I think you do see a certain amount, but you were also blindsided by this," Brody suggested. "And I'm not so sure something else wasn't going on that dulled your senses too."

"Like what?" Terk asked, looking at him, as they walked out to the truck.

"I don't know," Brody admitted. "I really don't, but it's something that I've been thinking about. I mean, for you to not see it, something must have been going on."

"Again, you're trying to make excuses for me," Terk pointed out, "and I don't think I deserve them."

"I can tell you one thing, Terk," Brody stated, "you don't deserve any of the blame. You didn't do this to us, and whoever the hell did are the ones who need to pay."

"Oh, I agree with you there," Terk confirmed. "But getting them to pay? … That'll be a whole different story. I would just as soon make sure that we were free and clear and capable of walking out."

"That's not a bad way to look at it either," Brody agreed, "if it's possible."

"I hope so. I really do because, otherwise, we'll have an

even harder road ahead."

Once in the truck, Brody felt a certain amount of relief flooding his system. His earlier distress left. He turned to Terk. "Just being out here again—I know it's stupid, and we just sat in the parked truck—but there's a sense of freedom, a sense of being back," he said with emphasis.

"And I get that too." Terk smiled at him. "There is that sense of having the team back together now. Having you back in the fold is finally pulling everything together."

Immediately Brody nodded. "That's what I mean. It was as if I was on the outside and struggling to find a way to fit back in with everybody to move forward. … I feel like I missed out on so much."

"Agreed," Terk murmured. "Now the trick is to make sure that nothing sets you back again."

"That would be rough," Brody admitted. "I'm feeling so much better, but I know I haven't been out of the coma for very long."

Terk snorted. "No, not very long at all. And every standard medical professional out there would have you recuperating at a much slower pace."

"And yet," Brody replied, "this is how I feel I can successfully recover. It feels like anything else would just hold me back."

"Maybe it would," Terk added. "We're giving this a try. So long as we don't overdo it, hopefully you'll be okay today."

"I better be," Brody murmured. "I know it takes time, but, Jesus, I'm not the most patient of people."

Terk snorted. "You think?" he teased. "Hopefully, when we return today, you'll remember that and integrate yourself into the group again, instead of feeling like you're on the outside."

Brody lapsed into silence, thinking that over. And Terk was right; Brody had held himself separate, apart from the team. Mostly because so much had happened without him, and they all seemed to be functioning at a level that he wanted to function at, but he didn't even know how to join in. He'd missed out on so much.

He was happy for all his friends, but it also left a gap in their connection. And it would be up to him to fill that gap again. He knew he was more than welcome here, and that had been made obvious, but the sense of being a part of the group, of being one of them, just hadn't happened yet. Still he'd hardly been here long enough for that.

He pondered that, right up until they pulled into a large warehouse building. "Where are we?" he asked.

"First, we'll pick up some of the deliveries that have been shipped over. More security cameras and Bluetooth headsets for everybody, so we can keep in touch when we're out," he murmured. "I'll be right back."

And, with that, Terk hopped out and disappeared inside. Only a few minutes later he came back out with several large boxes stacked up high. Immediately Brody hopped out and helped him load everything into the back of their vehicle. "What's next?" he asked, when Terk hopped back inside.

"Now we go to a commercial warehouse for groceries," he said. "Mariana has phoned in our order there, so, with any luck, we shouldn't have to wait long."

"So not even a grocery store?"

"We'll have to do that too but afterward," Terk explained. "We get the bulk of our stuff at the restaurant supply house now, but some of it has to come from warehouses."

And, with that, Terk drove to another location. Brody stayed outside again, watching as Terk took careful note of the surroundings and then slipped inside—obviously wary and not quite so comfortable with whatever was going on. Brody murmured to himself, "We can get through this."

Wary was good; wary was sensible, but it also meant that Brody needed to be doing his part too. And that was a little bit disconcerting because, up until then, nothing had even triggered that thought process in him.

As he waited, Brody watched as other vehicles pulled in. Several people loaded up and took off, and nothing stood out to him. Brody saw no sign of Terk yet. Just when Brody got antsy, wondering if he should go in and take a look for himself, Terk stepped outside.

He walked over to the truck. "That took a little longer than I expected. Sorry about that."

"I was just wondering if I was supposed to send in a search party," Brody joked. "I was thinking about storming the castle."

"It's all good. They were waiting to unload some stuff."

No signs of distress from Terk, not yet anyway. "So?" Brody prodded.

"We'll drive around to the back, and they'll load it up." And that's what they did.

It blew Brody away when they had everything loaded. "Now that's a lot of groceries."

"Well, that's what it's like feeding sixteen people three meals a day all the time," Terk murmured.

"Amazing," Brody said. "I wonder how Levi and Ice do it."

"With lots of help." Terk laughed. "And a lot of commitment from the people they have there."

"Agreed," he murmured. "And you've seen it in action many times, haven't you?"

"I have." Terk nodded. "It was something I considered setting up at one point in time, but it never really occurred to me that I could do it, not when we were all still working for the government."

"Well, we're not now." Brody curiously looked at his friend. "Would you reconsider now?"

"Maybe," he said calmly. "We're just not there yet."

And no way to argue with that. Until this attack on the team was settled, they wouldn't be planning much of anything regarding their future.

They made three more stops, where, once again, the groceries were either loaded or Terk went inside and picked them up.

Brody was curious about something and needed to get this out of the way, so, when Terk hopped in after the next shop, he asked him, "By the way, why is it you're doing this and not somebody else?"

"Because everybody else has something else to do, for one thing." Then he admitted simply, "I'm also checking to see how you're doing."

Brody winced at that. "Wow, so this is kind of babysitting duty."

"Well, if it was babysitting, it wouldn't be half as much fun. And I can do this, so why not?" Terk murmured, as he looked out the window. "Everybody else takes on so much of the laborious work that it makes me feel bad. So I help with things as I can."

Brody stared at Terk. "Good God, I have never had a thought like that. Neither has anyone else, and that is something I'm certain of."

"No, maybe not," Terk agreed, "but, at the same time, there is always something to do, and our people are good about jumping in to get things done. And it doesn't have to be the job that we think it'll be. I'm totally okay to do my part. My team needs to see it."

"That's the trick, isn't it?" Brody said. "We all do something to help out in any way we can to make it all run smoothly."

"Exactly." Terk smiled, as he motioned at the parking lot he was pulling into.

"Where are we now?"

"We have a delivery from Charles," he said, smiling.

"Really? What's he sending over?"

"Hopefully not MI6," Terk stated in a dry tone. "I may have worn out my welcome there."

"Do we ever get a welcome anywhere?" Brody asked curiously.

"Not really. Not if you ask me. But it's all good."

Except that, when Terk went inside, he didn't come back out for a long time.

Brody was getting frustrated. Frowning and fussing in the vehicle, he finally gave up and hopped out, moving closer to the building, and slipped up to the corner near a side door.

He waited there, listening for any sound or anyone out of place around him. When he heard nothing, he immediately contacted Calum. "I'm not sure what's going on," Brody explained, "but Terk went into the building, where he's supposedly picking up stuff from Charles, and it's been a while."

"Shit," Cal said. "That'll be MI6 trying to screw something up."

"Well, they don't really get that option, do they?"

"No, not necessarily, but you know those guys don't give a shit either."

"I can stay out here and wait, or I can go in and attempt to mount a rescue," Brody suggested. "Do you have any way to contact Terk?"

"Contacting Terk if he was open to being contacted would be easy," Calum replied, "but he's not showing that he's open to communication."

Brody was astonished to hear that. "If that's the case, I feel like I need to go in there."

"Depends on whether Charles is even there," Calum noted. "Give me a second to check, and I'll get back to you." And, with that, the call was disconnected.

When Calum phoned him back not even three minutes later, he said, "Charles says to go in there, and, if there's a problem, and you don't contact me in the next few minutes, Charles will be all over it."

"Good enough." Brody turned the corner and headed toward the side door. Instinct had him stepping back, just as he was about to open the door. Good timing as the door opened in front of him, and two men came outside, talking.

Terk was not one of them. Brody had already slipped into the alcove and watched the pair closely. They headed away from Brody and got into a vehicle. Brody waited until they disappeared and slipped inside the same door.

As he stealthily walked in, he tried hard to keep his presence hidden. If MI6 had any kind of security cameras, Brody would have been picked up already. As he walked forward, he heard Terk's voice.

"You really don't want to be doing this," he said.

"We're a little damn tired of you guys," said one guy,

disgust in his voice. "Plus you keep leaving us bodies."

"Oh, do I now?" Terk asked. "And here I thought it was the bad guys killing other bad guys. You don't really know which side you're on, do you?"

"I know which side I'm on," the one guy stated, "and I'm tired of you fucking around with my government."

"Interesting," Terk noted, but absolutely no inflection filled his voice.

Brody was about to go in when Terk stepped into his brain, and the message was clear as day. *Stay out.*

Brody hesitated at that, unsure if Terk was maybe telling Brody to stay out for his own safety, which would piss him right off. He waited in the shadows and started recording the conversation. He wasn't sure who was pulling the strings right now, but it sure as hell didn't sound like this meeting was on the up-and-up.

Terk's team had seen that time and time again too. Some asshole figured that they should have been in on something and wanted payback for it.

When the guy came back at Terk again, he was snarling. "And why the hell shouldn't we just take you out right now?" he asked, his tone full of venom.

"Wow, that'd be totally illegal for MI6, would it not?" Terk laughed. "Or do you guys work outside the law now?"

"I don't give a shit if it's legal or not," he snapped. "You're making a mockery out of us all."

"Nope, I can't do that. If you're not the idiots you're currently pretending to be here," Terk stated, "feel free to contact your superiors about this."

"Well, I guess what our superiors don't know," he said, "won't matter. Sometimes you have to be a little more proactive, and we have a lot of leeway in our jobs."

"You seem to, indeed," Terk noted in such a calm voice.

Brody had a detached sense of wonder hearing the agent, obviously some midlevel man, beyond pissed at what was going on. Clearly this guy wasn't sure he had any recourse for the accusations he was flinging about, and that was probably making him feel all the more impotent and frustrated.

Terk's team came across this every once in a while, with somebody who thought that they should be somebody bigger or somebody better or somebody who could change the way things were being handled. Sometimes it worked; sometimes it didn't.

Brody hoped this guy got his knuckles rapped. Or better yet, taken down more than a few pegs. *This guy is dangerous.*

He sent Terk a warning, but his friend was clearly in control. The guy was a loose cannon, one of the ones destined to go off on his own and without a thought about his team. That kind of maverick attitude was not helpful when it came to an organization like this.

Brody wondered how long it would take before somebody from upper management got wind of what this agent was planning on doing on his own.

Not that Brody cared, as long as the loose cannon guy let Terk leave.

When Terk spoke next, his voice was calm as a sunny day. "I'm walking out of here right now, but I'll be sure to pass on your concerns."

The guy snorted. "What makes you think you're walking anywhere?" he asked, his voice turning deadly.

At that, Brody stiffened and approached even more quietly. This was not the kind of behavior they expected, and something was definitely going on here. Still recording, he edged even closer, so he could just barely see where Terk stood next to a closed door on the opposite wall.

As they came into focus, Terk was smiling at the guy. "Are you ready to do this right now? You've got two henchmen with you. Local agency grunts?" he asked in a mildly curious voice.

One of the guys asked, "Hey, who are you calling a grunt?" His tone had a deadly note to it. "You're operating illegally in this country. We could take you out, and nobody would ask any questions."

At that, Terk laughed. "In that case, you should have done it already. Now I'm leaving, so, if you're planning on stopping me, I suggest you grab that gun out of your holster and put it to good use. Otherwise you and I will have something to talk about later."

"What will you do? Run and say something to our bosses?" he asked in a mocking voice. "Do you really think we haven't thought of all that?"

"I'm sure you have at some point," Terk replied calmly. "And I really don't care about complaining to bosses. I know who they will believe already, and it sure as hell isn't you."

Brody checked their expressions when they all went quiet. A moment of shared consternation.

"I don't know what you're talking about," the lead guy snapped. "And, if you mean that washed-up old soldier Charles, you're barking up the wrong tree. It's well past time that he retired too."

"Ah," Terk noted with interest. "You're now threatening Charles's life? That'll go over really well. Charles has devoted his entire life to your country and now look at you." Terk was egging on these guys. "You're mocking somebody who has done more in service than you could ever dream of. All you're thinking about is yourselves."

"We are not," one man protested. "We're thinking about our country."

"No, you're not. This has nothing to do with your country. This is all about you guys making sure that you're noticed and *big men* in the company," Terk said in a mocking tone. "That's all this is. It's a power move, hoping you can make a move further up. I'm sure you'll try to make my death look like somebody else in the company was responsible, right? That's always a good ploy, isn't it?"

The other guy looked uneasily at his friends. "We're doing this because we need to. Nobody else will listen to us and this needs to be done."

"Maybe there's a reason why nobody listens to you," Terk stated, with half a smile.

"Why the hell are you so damn cocky about this anyway?" the head guy asked uncertainly. "It's not as if you've got any way to get out of this."

Terk looked at him, bored. "What makes you think I need a way to get out of this?" he asked. "You guys have no frickin' clue." He succeeded at making them feel uneasy, questioning their plan. "That's the problem with being a low-level grunt and a midlevel wannabe."

He looked from the guy in charge to the other two. "You've not been clued in to the intricacies of life above you because they already know you can't be trusted. MI6 already knows that you're not worthy of moving up a step and that you'll never be what you thought you would be. That's probably what brought this on. Chances are you guys were given your walking papers or at least a warning about not trespassing where you don't belong." Terk snorted. "And, like typical grunts, you couldn't take that message and carry on your merry way."

"Stop calling us that," one guy yelled at Terk. "We've devoted years to this outfit. They've got no business shutting us down."

"You have to earn your promotion to move up a position," Terk stated. "And this? … This just earned you all kinds of black marks. But that's all right, keep going, and we'll see just how far you're willing to go in pursuit of what you think is good for *the company*." He air quoted the phrase, clearly grating on them.

"He's awfully confident." The second guy spoke up for the first time. "I don't like this. Let's be done with it."

"That's just the kind of assholes they are," the head guy replied. "Americans. … Nothing but pigs."

"This is not about him. It's about all the injustices that he keeps perpetrating on our soil. We have to do what we need to do to keep our people safe."

At that, even Brody was surprised. It was really pushing boundaries to make it sound like Terk had done anything against England.

The fact was, the assholes who had attacked Terk's team were already here on their soil. Some of them surely came from other places, but they were all one, and they could travel as freely as they wanted.

Even being on a no-fly list didn't stop known criminals from traveling, since, with private planes, they could travel anywhere. So anything they wanted was easy and simple for them, as long as they had lots of cash. Regardless, the allegations against Terk here were a complete distortion of the facts.

Just then, Brody heard somebody approaching. He quickly stepped behind a pillar to stay out of the way. Yet now he had people on both sides of him. Potential enemies. They may or may not see him, depending on whether they turned and looked in his direction or not.

He immediately pulled up an energy screen, trying to block anybody from seeing him. The pillar had a side mirror, and, looking at himself, he realized just how shaky he was and how damn thin.

Shocked and horrified, he pulled harder and harder, trying to find a way to make that energy a little bit stronger and to keep as still as possible to keep hidden. *I am not up to this shit now.*

He suddenly realized just how weak he felt and how much danger he was in. Without thinking, almost in a panic, he sent out an SOS. He contacted Clary to help him build his energy shield.

With no questions asked, Clary sent energy, suddenly flowing through his veins. He quickly managed to pull himself up in an energy field and to create an energy shield that would block him from anybody approaching.

And just in time. Somebody came through, looked once in his direction, and kept on walking out the same door Brody had entered. He let out a shaky breath as he realized the shield had worked.

Not on his own but with help from her.

He realized just how much more he owed her.

Just doing my job, big guy.

He winced at that because, God, how cold and formal was that? But he was also the one who had put them on that footing. He needed to do something about that but not right now.

Right now he needed to focus. Terk was in danger. Keeping the energy as a strong shield around him, Brody stepped forward until he was through the room, almost to Terk, without being seen by these three fools.

One of the grunts looked in his direction and then looked away, not even seeing him. And that's how good the camouflage was, which was worth its weight in gold. *Bear with me, Clary. Terk is in trouble.*

By the time he stepped forward, almost right up beside Terk, nobody had noticed anything. This shield was stronger and more intense than anything Brody had ever produced before. It was fascinating, but he didn't have time to think about that.

Terk looked over in his direction, and Brody saw the surprise on his face, but it was quickly masked. Terk turned, looked at his captors. "So, do I leave without a fuss or do we have a problem right now?"

"We have a problem," the first man said, pulling out his gun. He looked at his two cohorts. "John has gone and he was the last one in the building. Let's get ready, and we'll take him out, ambush-style."

"And our report?"

"We'll write it up that he attacked us because we were questioning him too closely. It's obvious he was losing it and went off his rocker," he explained casually.

Just the fact that he was willing to put that level of deception into this made him all the more dangerous. Standing beside Terk, completely hidden, was one of the most freeing aspects that Brody had ever experienced before. But he also knew that he couldn't sustain it much longer.

He walked around behind the first man and just as he raised his weapon, he hit him hard.

Now the report will be more accurate, asshole.

CHAPTER 7

CLARY HELD THE energy firm and strong, as she tried to sort out what was going on.

She heard voices around her and her own sister telling the team to be quiet. "Something's happening."

Clary knew her sister. Cara was picking up some of what was going on. But it was all about trying to keep Brody safe. And obviously that would be a little more difficult than Clary had thought, when he could find danger in grocery shopping.

Bringing him back here to his team, where he was even more exposed to this gigantic mess threatening them, would bite her in the ass. But she hadn't really thought this through. She had seen the sense of bringing him back into the fold, as it would calm him somewhat, and it would keep him connected, and the group could help him revive his spirit, but this was too much.

The group obviously cared about him. They were a family and would make all attempts to try and connect him back to life. She just hadn't expected this ambush.

When she had finally tried to shake out of Brody's system, again, more trouble brewed. But she didn't have any context. She was shaking when her sister quietly showed up at her side. "Do you need help?"

She gave a light headshake. She didn't waste the energy

trying to answer her. It was not as clean-cut or as simple as she would have liked it to be. But, as it was, something was going on.

"We have others on it," Cara confirmed, then gave a nod.

Clary kept her eyes closed and her energy focused on Brody. She sensed a sudden shift, and then she received a heavy blow. She was alarmed at the drain of energy. *I need to shut this down.*

Her instincts were to keep him safe, and she was considering shutting him down, but the drain of energy suggested Brody was under attack. She was serious about saying that she would shut him down for his own good, but this felt different.

But right now he was functioning with her energy, and that wasn't something that she had really thought about. Whatever was happening was obviously important. She wished she knew what it was. She just didn't have a clue what was going on.

The drain suddenly stopped. She let herself slowly breathe, as the energy calmed and then dissipated down to a fine thread. She opened her eyes to see the group watching her anxiously. Clary shrugged. "I'm not exactly sure what's going on, but something became a massive stressor on Brody, and then it stopped."

"Is he okay?" Tasha asked anxiously. "Is Brody okay?"

"Brody is okay," she murmured. "So is Terk. As for what just happened, I'm really not exactly sure. I only get impressions. Some kind of a dispute and, other than that, I'm not sure."

"Clary?"

She felt a hand on her shoulder, looked over at her sister,

and smiled. "Interesting times. It's very strange here," she murmured, "and not what we're used to."

"No."

"I'm not exactly sure how to handle it."

"You'll work it out," Cara noted. "How did he do?"

"He did decently," Clary replied, "but something odd happened." She hesitated, knowing other people were around. She lowered her voice and explained, then Cara's eyebrows shot up.

"Now that is interesting." Cara glanced over at Rick and asked, "I suppose that camouflage works?"

He looked at her, then at Clary. "He was able to use your energy though?"

Clary nodded.

"That is good news." Rick rubbed his hands together. "He provides an essential skill for us that nobody else has been able to develop."

"I don't understand the camouflage," Clary admitted.

"He has the ability to pull energy from around us to help camouflage us. Like we're there, but no one can see us. Normally he can only do it on the spot, with one other person assisting him. Yet he has always said that he felt he had the ability to go further and deeper with that skill, but we didn't have a chance to get any more training. The fact that he has managed to do it, so soon after coming out of the coma, is amazing. Also the fact that he managed to turn to you for that energy that he was missing is even more impressive." he stated. "I can see that, from your perspective, it's all kind of weird, but it is, in this case, wonderful."

Cara eyed her sister intently.

Clary nodded. "I think part of the thing that got me was the fact that he wasn't even hesitant when he asked for the energy. Then, when it was there, he used it. That showed a level of skill and an acceptance that surprised me." She wore a huge smile. "I'm not used to seeing too many other people work with energy."

"And yet here we all do, including our partners to some extent," Rick confirmed. "So that will be for the two of you to work out. I know from experience that it isn't all roses."

More like guns and roses. Clary nodded. "Brody's not there yet."

"I get that," Rick acknowledged, "but obviously he's not far off." And, with that, he bounced to his feet and disappeared.

Clary shook her head at her sister. "I don't know if Brody can do this all the time."

"You can't worry about that," Cara stated. "These guys have abilities that we've never seen before. They can handle it on their own."

"This is so strange," Clary said. "It never really occurred to me, although we've discussed it, as you know, half-heartedly over the last decade. We said that maybe we would find somebody like us, but we never really expected it to happen. Or at least I didn't. Of course there's Terk, but he's in a class of his own."

"I didn't expect it for me either," Cara declared. "When I felt Brody out there, that was one of the reasons why I contacted you to help. I didn't know how deep I could go, when I was already connected in many ways to Rick."

"Right," Clary agreed. "It's a fascinating thought."

"It's fascinating, scary, and concerning, almost debilitating in a way," Cara replied, "because, as we know, once you start to care, it affects your judgment."

"Right, and that was something I was trying not to do

because, of course, I intend to keep helping other people."

"Of course you are. So am I," Cara said, "and I am getting better at compartmentalizing it."

"Are you?" Clary asked her sister in surprise. "It is possible then?"

"It is definitely possible." Cara smiled. "And I get that you know we'll have an awful lot to work on here and a lot that we ourselves will have to improve on." She touched her sister's cheek. "However, we can do this."

"So I will still help other patients?" The relief Clary felt at that was amazing. She sagged in place. "You have no idea how worried I was that, once I connected on this level, I wouldn't have a life of my own again," she continued. "I worried that I couldn't do the work that I care about so much."

Cara nodded. "I think it'll all be there for us, and, in many ways, we might even be stronger. I wondered too, you know? In other words, this has been a really positive learning experience for you. Right?"

"Absolutely," Clary said, smiling.

"I think it's important for you to remember that. We are not in any way inhibited by these deeper connections happening between me and Rick or with you and Brody," Cara stated. "I think we will become comfortable enough to realize that whatever is happening is a good thing."

"Well, I hope so," Clary added, "because, so far, it doesn't really feel that way."

Cara chuckled. "Nope, I'm sure it doesn't. But that doesn't mean that we won't get there."

Clary smiled at her sister. "That's definitely making me feel a little bit better though."

"Good." Cara nodded. "Now, are you up for some food?

You haven't eaten very much since you got here, and you make me worry."

Clary laughed. "I could use a bite, as long as they won't call on me again. I might throw up."

"And I can't guarantee that," Cara shared, "because, whatever happened just now, it will be happening more and more. Yet we'll never really know all the details, unless you tune in to that level."

At that, Sophia, who had sat down beside them, asked curiously, "Can you tune into that level so that you can see what's happening?"

"If we try hard, yes," Clary replied. "We normally do it on the other plane though." With the confusion on Sophia's face, Clary explained, "When people are crossing over, we tend to tune in at that time and ensure that they are crossing safely and not stuck in-between."

Cara pitched in, "It's tuning into a level of just soul or spirit energy, whatever you call it."

Clary nodded and continued. "In essence, without the spirit, there's nothing left in the physical body, and we are attached only to the residual energy there. So we attempt to connect both body and soul by tapping into the energy."

Sophia stared at them both, clearly stunned. "And all of that sounds absolutely incredible," she murmured.

Clary smiled at her. "After everything you've seen and heard here?" she asked, with a hint of confusion.

Sophia laughed. "I have had my eyes opened so much since I arrived here. However, what you can do is scary though, and I am in no way jealous. I would not want that much pressure on me to help save a life."

She clearly had more on her mind than just this.

Sophia continued. "It's bad enough when it's a pressure

that we put on ourselves here. We're expected to try and save our friends when we're out on missions. So to think that you could do something, while you are sitting right here in front of me, is like, ... it's just amazing." She added heartily, "I'm grateful that you're here and that I can see it too."

Clary grimaced. "And I wouldn't want the responsibility of trying to save any life on an actual mission in the way that you speak of."

"I guess we each do what we can offer, huh?" Sophia noted.

Clary was lost in her thoughts. "Life is sacred for us, but I do wonder. It's not always enough."

At that, Sophia nodded. "Sometimes there's just nothing you can do. So we still have to do our best and hope that everything works out." With that, she got a call from Tasha at the computers. Sophia walked back over to her station, and the conversation was left to just the two sisters.

"Have you really felt like you can fit in here?" Clary asked her sister.

"I have," Cara softly replied. "I know it probably seems odd and not necessarily something you would have expected, but good people are here."

"I'm sure there are." Clary looked around. "That is very clear just from the energy alone." She smiled, looking over at the group of them, deep in discussion.

"Exactly," Cara agreed. "I have to admit, when you look at the energy around here, it's pretty fierce, loving, caring, and there's an awful lot of good things about it."

"I'll take your word for it," Clary replied. "Right now, my head is killing me, and, besides, ... I'm not quite there yet."

"You will be," Cara stated quietly. "I know you will.

And not just because I want you close by," she added. "As sisters go, of course we want to be in each other's lives."

She was gearing up for something sensitive, and Clary could see it.

"But with the type of energy work we do, the type of trust that we have in each other, I think it makes it even more important that we're in a similar situation."

"Maybe, but you can't force personal relationships to happen," Clary noted, "and I'm not in any position right now to even want to do something like that."

"Of course not," Cara agreed. "Yet I have faith. I trust that something will work out." She nodded.

"Maybe. We'll see."

Cara just chuckled. "That was always you too," she said, "not so much the doubting Thomas but always leery. Always waiting to see what would happen. You used to have more faith in people."

"Been burned before," Clary said.

"I have a hunch it'll be different this time," Cara murmured. "He's different."

"He is?" Clary gave an eye roll. "Cranky and not exactly easy to get along with? You are mad."

"Are you?" she asked curiously.

She glared at her sister. "No, I'm not. That's part of my point. Given every interaction so far, it appears that we aren't suited."

"I think you're well past that point," Cara argued, "and I don't think you could have gotten to where you are without seeing something better than that in Brody. And yet who knows?"

"Maybe we can find out all kinds of new things about each other later, and it will be at a completely different level."

"Maybe," Cara murmured.

"We'll just have to see."

"The joy of the journey is what's important right now."

"Well, if he was fully healed and surviving on his own maybe," Clary stated, "but he isn't. So the journey itself isn't all that smooth yet."

"No, but you'll do what you need to do to keep him alive and well," Cara stated, "because that's who we are."

For now.

TERK LOOKED AT Brody incredulously. "How did that feel?"

"After knocking him on his ass? Perfect," Brody replied. "Feeling back in control of my life and having some control over the situation felt really good. The ability to do something and to be of use was priceless."

"That's not what I was asking but …"

Brody looked over at his boss and grinned. "It worked even easier than I thought it would. Maybe I'm fully healed."

Terk immediately shook his head. "No. You are not. You're forgetting one big factor in this success."

"What's that?" Brody dragged his attention from the three unconscious men on the ground back to Terk. "Why do you say that?"

"You're forgetting Clary."

"I'm not forgetting her"—Brody tried to hide his face from Terk—"I just kept hoping that she wouldn't interfere."

At that, Terk smiled. "Well, she didn't interfere, not like stopping you, and, for that … you do need to give her some credit."

"I do, and the thing is, I don't even know exactly how much was her and how much was me," Brody stated. "I'm still trying to puzzle my way out of it."

"Good," Terk noted. "Puzzle away because it's fascinating. I'm not sure how that came to be, but it looked like you needed energy, and she provided it."

"And that's a good way to look at it," Brody said. "It was just bizarre. I needed it, and I …" He stopped. "I kind of thought about asking for it, … or maybe I did. I don't know, but suddenly it was just … there." He turned to look at Terk even closer. "That was her. Wasn't it?"

"You tell me. How much of it was her?"

Brody could already see the answer on Terk's face. "It really was her. *All* of it. … Jesus," Brody mumbled. "I'm really surprised at how smooth that flow of energy was. Like she's a pro."

"She *is* a pro," Terk reminded him.

Brody didn't appreciate that though. "You just had to remind me, didn't you?"

"She heals, Brody. She doesn't do warfare."

He nodded. "Got it, … or at least I'm trying to remind myself of that. She was very talented in how quickly she managed to participate."

"That's because her energy flows through you even now. She managed to find you when you were unconscious and completely out of our reach on the ethers. She knows you, at the soul level, and you are running off her energy to a degree already." Terk looked more closely at Brody and nodded. "I can see it, but you haven't really noticed her energy constantly thrumming through you yourself, have you?"

"That's because it feels like my energy," Brody admitted, with some frustration. "It's hard to separate the two."

"Agreed." Terk nodded. "And I think that's an important point. Consider that. It is quite possible that it may not be something that you can separate."

Brody stared at his friend, frowning. "Meaning?" He hated the ominous tone of his voice, but, if somebody had told him something like that, it was guaranteed to have an immediate effect on him.

"Meaning," Terk replied, "that there's definitely a flow of energy between the two of you that frankly is magical to watch."

"Stop it, man. You are embarrassing me."

"It'll take time, but soon you'll see it for yourself."

Brody knew Terk was right. Brody could almost see her energy now. "I suppose I will."

"You need to come to some sort of understanding."

Brody knew that Terk was asking him to be vigilant, and Brody understood that at least. He thought about it and had a realization. "I guess I just utilized her energy without even thinking about it. It was there. I needed it, and I took it." He frowned at himself. "I've never been in that situation before."

"Nope," Terk agreed, "but I have. It's something that I have to do regularly, depending on where we're at as a team. Yet you must understand the ramifications too. Interesting that it's now something that faces you. You need to pay more attention. It is good, but it can be very bad if abused."

"I don't know about *interesting*, and honestly *bad* sounds more like it," he murmured. Right then he turned to face Terk. "Is it the same thing for Cara and Rick?"

"It's possible," Terk noted. "I haven't asked them specifically."

"Well, maybe we should talk about that," Brody murmured. "It does seem a little bit odd to consider that this is something that's part of our new world now."

"But," Terk added, "you have to realize that Cara has made the decision to stay with us. Cara and Rick are a couple, and to ask them something personal can get very awkward, very fast. On the other hand, I'm not sure about Clary. She was hired to keep you alive, and she stayed and came to the compound because it's part of that job. And, if there's one thing I have learned, it's that these women are incredibly ethical. Until they're satisfied that you'll be okay on your own, they are not leaving."

"I got a similar impression too," Brody confirmed. "In a way, they're kind of scary."

Terk burst out laughing. "Considering what they can do, that's probably not a bad thing. A little bit of healthy respect can keep a lot of people in line."

"I understand, but we need to ask. It affects me, and it will affect the team, when you think about it."

"Sure."

"They *are* pretty badass." Brody stared at Terk now.

"Yeah, but the minute you cross them, I wouldn't want to be in your shoes."

Brody winced at that. "I feel like all I've done is cross her. At least, butt heads with her."

"It's part and parcel of it, I think," Terk said. "You obviously have a lot of relationship stuff there to work out."

"I wouldn't look at it like that," Brody argued in frustration. "That's not what I was thinking at all."

"Maybe not, but maybe you need to think about it," Terk suggested.

"I don't do relationships," Brody declared instantly.

Terk burst out laughing again. "Doesn't matter if you do or don't. You do now, whether you like it or not."

Brody glared at him. "That's not funny."

"Of course not," Terk said, "but there is absolutely no way that you can stand here and tell me that she doesn't matter to you."

Brody felt an unsettling knowing inside. "No, I guess I can't."

"Exactly. Because she *does* mean something to you, and that's not a bad thing. The fact that she does mean something to you also is important because we don't know where and how this will end. If she means something to you, you'll also help look after her. It's a partnership, and you will help keep her safe through all this."

"I hadn't really considered that either," he muttered. "I can't though. Not right now." He stared out in the distance and then looked down at the men on the ground. "So, will we just stand here with these idiots, or is there a plan?"

Just then Terk's phone buzzed. He looked at the message, smiled. "Nope. Safe to leave now."

"Wait. … Why? Why are we leaving these douchebags here like this?" Brody asked in surprise. "I'm not comfortable with that."

"Neither am I," Terk noted. "However, Charles has offered to step in, and he'll take care of it."

"Even though he's on their shit list?"

"Maybe *because* he's on their shit list," Terk replied. "We do have to give the guy a chance to deal with the bad apples in his own house."

"I guess," Brody agreed, "but these guys won't stop anytime soon."

"Nope, they won't," Terk said picking up their bags, "but I think Charles knows that it's his problem."

Brody walked back outside and asked Terk, "Where to

now?"

"Well, this stop took a little bit longer than I thought it would," Terk noted. "And considering we have ice cream in the truck, I say we better head straight home."

"Ice cream?" he muttered, as he shook his head. "Who would have thought that ice cream would ever be dictating our actions?"

At that, Terk burst out laughing again. "Oh my God, it is so good to have you guys up and alive and doing well."

"I guess it was pretty rough for a while there, wasn't it?"

"It was more than rough," he admitted. "Jesus, knowing that our friends were all suffering, and I could only do a limited amount for any of you was pretty painful."

"Sorry, but thanks for keeping me alive and for hiring both Clary and Cara."

"Not an issue," he said. "You know I'd do it again in a heartbeat."

And that's the thing—because they were friends and they worked in the same field and they did the same things—Brody knew that's exactly what Terk would do. "I still don't understand why you didn't go down," Brody noted.

"I'm not sure about that either," he murmured. "And that's something I'm trying to get to the bottom of. I think it was EMP related and short circuited my energy. In a way saving me."

"Any update on Celia?"

"Not yet." Terk sighed heavily. "Ice tells me that she's awake but still doesn't appear to remember anything. I'll have to check in on her, but I haven't really had the energy to do so."

"In what way would you check on her?"

"I want to know if she's cognitively all there or if they've done something else to her. Physically she's getting better …"

"Ouch. That would be pretty rough."

"You have no idea," Terk said. "These guys are assholes, and their minions are dropping like flies around us. But there's always more assholes to take their place. We need to come to a happy ending with this on a permanent basis. I've had more than enough trouble getting them to stop their attacks on us. Just how does Texas connect? At the moment the circumstances appear to be completely unrelated, but that hardly seems possible."

Brody understood that Terk's frustration knew no bounds.

Terk added, "The time is right, now to put an end to it. They can't hurt you guys anymore, and that's what I've been waiting for. So now I highly suggest we put a permanent end to these guys."

"I'm right there with you," Brody stated. "I'm beyond pissed that I got cut out of the loop as it is."

Terk laughed. "You've hardly been cut out of the loop, so don't exaggerate."

Brody grinned at his friend. "Says you. I didn't get a chance to do anything with all those other assholes you guys were fighting. You know I would have been right in there, helping myself to some of that."

"And maybe gotten yourself in more trouble," Terk reminded him. "Yet now you appear to have a guardian angel, who steps in whenever you need it."

"Yeah, and how the hell did that ever happen? To both me and Rick apparently," he murmured.

"I know, and that's something else that makes all of us

sit up and wonder." Terk hesitated.

Brody picked up on that, felt he had earned the right to know the truth, uncensored. "What?"

Terk nodded, obviously deciding to explain further here. "Damon said that Tasha's skills are developing too, and, with both of them in a relationship and working all the time with each other, I'm not surprised."

"She already was a hell of an admin for us. And we still need her with us, but the fact that she's picking up and doing more and learning more about the energy work is also good for her—and us—as well."

As they got back into the truck, Brody watched as Charles pulled up alongside them, walked over, talked to them.

"I got the gist of what went on," Charles noted, "but not all of it. So, do you mind filling me in?"

"I have a recording if you want," Brody offered. Terk looked at Brody in surprise, and he shrugged. "I was recording it as it was happening." He didn't need to clarify, but he still did. "I wasn't sure what your game plan was, Terk, so I just waited, as you had asked me to stay out of it."

"I would very much like a copy of that," Charles stated. "It would help me to deal with these people effectively."

"Good luck with that," Brody said. "First, you'll have to wake them up."

Charles looked at them in alarm. "Did you hurt them?"

"No, not at all," Brody confirmed, "but they might not remember everything when they do wake up."

"Why?" Charles asked.

"It is a common side effect of an energy knockout."

Charles winced. "I can't have you hurting them. However, I get that, in this case, it was self-defense. And believe me.

I'll be utilizing that to the best of my ability. People in this agency are against having you involved in any way. So, it would be great if you could avoid hurting them."

"Which is why I didn't," Brody stated. "I just knocked them out and kept them down."

"Good," Charles replied. "Much appreciated."

As Charles headed to pick up his three men, Brody pulled up his phone to send the recorded files to Charles. "Hope he can do something about these guys. Assholes like that really don't need to be on MI6's staff." Brody sounded off, worn out and haggard.

"Not only do they not need to be on staff, it would be better for us if they were nowhere near us," Terk added, also exhausted. "It just becomes a huge headache for us. When there are fighting factions within the same department, shit always hits the fan."

"It isn't there always, though," Brody noted.

"No, hopefully not always," Terk agreed. "That's one of the reasons why we have to do what we're doing. We need to ensure that we don't have tunnel vision about our government putting this on us. We have other potential suspects."

"Have you mentioned that to Charles at all?"

"Yes, and he's looking into it on the side," Terk said. "It's just that trying to get answers isn't exactly the easiest thing. These assholes after us have been hiring local guns, then covering their tracks, and nobody's really left to talk to."

Terk started the truck. "Let's go home. You can work on that whole relationship thing with Clary." A hint of laughter filled his voice, as Terk turned the vehicle back in the direction of home.

CHAPTER 8

WHEN BRODY WALKED in, Clary watched him carefully, looking to see if he was in any way affected. She knew her sister, Cara, was doing the same thing. But he looked good, given that the last energy draw was substantial. He not only looked comparatively healthy but vibrant. Although to the trained medical eye, he was still recovering.

There was a sense of confidence, almost cockiness back in his step though. He'd been able to do something effectively, and that had made a huge difference in his demeanor.

She was loving that.

Nothing like seeing somebody come back to life and helping out in their own healing process. He wouldn't necessarily be thrilled with how she saw it, but he was doing a lot better.

Sometime soon he may not need her anymore.

She acknowledged that there would be a change in the near future, and that thought ... made her heart pang slightly. She was prepared to ignore it.

For now.

She was here for a job, not necessarily to stay. Yet just something about him strummed her heartstrings and pulled them in a big way. He was a special person, and, as she was starting to realize, a lot of people here depended on him. With the nightmare that they all found themselves in, they needed everyone banded together.

As he walked toward her, the others fell silent, as if watching and waiting. He looked down at her with uncertainty. "Thank you."

"You're welcome," she replied calmly. "Glad you're alive and well."

"Are you saying there would be a chance I shouldn't be?" he asked.

"With the amount of energy drawn, I was a bit worried and unsure. If I didn't shut you down at the right time," she explained, "there's always a chance that somebody could pop a bullet in you, and I wouldn't have a lifeline to keep you alive."

He stared at her, looking fascinated. "Could you really keep me alive in that situation?"

"Not necessarily," she admitted. "Every case is different, but I would hate to lose anybody now. I haven't handed you off yet, so it'll piss me off if I think I'll lose somebody ahead of time."

He chuckled. "Well, I'm grateful. It was kind of dicey there for a while."

"Message received on that part," she confirmed, "and apparently you're okay now." She was beyond curious.

He nodded. "Bad guys taken down. Charles is handling it now—or as much as anybody in the agency is allowed to handle it."

"Just what the hell was that anyway?" Damon asked, walking to him. He sounded almost as pissed as Brody had been at the time.

"Some midlevel MI6 operative and a couple of his henchmen were all of the opinion that Terk should be taken for a very short one-way walk for all his crimes against their country," Brody relayed chillingly. "I don't think they particularly gave a shit about the factual details," Brody stated, obviously venting, and they let him. "It was pretty frustrating because they had their own agenda, and they were quite happy to take out Charles too."

"That will get them in trouble more than anything," Terk noted. "Charles wields a ton of power, and, although he says he's retired, I'm not sure I believe it."

"I'm not sure either." Brody looked from one to the other. "Maybe he was, and maybe he's been brought back into service or something. I don't know, but, when it came down to it today, Charles was there to handle these three loose cannons."

"He has also gone to bat and vouched for us previously, several times," Terk added. "I would hate for anything to happen to him." They were all of the same mind. At that, Terk's phone rang. He smiled. "It's my brother. I better go take this." And he turned and walked away.

The others looked at Brody.

"Are you doing okay?" Damon asked.

"I'm doing great," Brody replied, with a smile. "It was really nice to have my brain intact and apparently functioning at a level I hadn't really been expected to function at for a long time." He looked happy and content. "I mean, it felt good. I don't know quite what's awaiting me, but I'm happy to report that I did okay out there."

Damon slapped him on the shoulder. "Good. We'll get some grub, once we get all this stuff put away, and maybe we can talk more then."

BRODY KNEW THAT Damon was curious to know more, but he probably figured it best to let it go for now. "I'd like that," Brody agreed. "I need to start pulling my weight for the team again."

"Anytime you're ready," Wade and Damon replied in unison, and it surprised Brody. "We've just been waiting for you, buddy." Wade patted him on the back.

They both turned and headed out, presumably to help unload all the groceries that had come back with them. But it was enough for Brody to realize that Terk had been correct. Brody'd been the one who was sitting out, when he could have been part of it.

The realization made him sad because, for some reason, he'd felt isolated when he woke up alone. Almost like an abandonment. Maybe that had been his doing. At least now he was back and feeling solid again.

He looked over to see Clary studying him. "What?" he asked, frowning at her. "You always look at me like I'm a unicorn."

"Surprise." She nodded. "That's because you are. You have to understand that my sister and I, … we read energy—and have done so for a long time. But we haven't had much exposure to others who can wield energy the way you guys do. So, when you put out the call for more energy, you surprised me. I didn't have a problem giving it to you," she continued, "but it was fascinating to watch you work it."

He nodded. "I wasn't even thinking when I put out the call for energy. It was just instinctive to ask for help, and it was there, just like that. I owe you a huge thanks for that."

"Maybe," Clary replied, "but it's the kind of work you do. So I guess that type of request is to be expected."

He smiled. "Yes, and no. There'll never be a point in

time when there isn't potential for things to go wrong."

She laughed. "No, you've got that right. But, for now, your thanks are accepted."

"Wow." He rubbed his stomach. "I need to get some food *now*."

"You do in a big way," she agreed, "and so do I."

He looked at her and frowned. "You mean, because of the work I did?"

"Yes, and I overexerted myself as well."

"I funneled away a ton of energy when I knocked those guys out."

"Yeah, well, that was my energy. Yours was already long gone when I intervened."

He burst out laughing. "In that case, come on. Let's head to the kitchen and get something to eat. You never know when I'll have to knock out the next guy."

AS SHE THOUGHT about it, she realized it was a lot different working with Brody than her usual patients.

It's not that it was bad; it was just different. She and Brody were both from different worlds, and everything about them was different. Looking around her, she realized that they were not like most people. Most people didn't acclimate or live in their own restricted space very well, but these people around her did.

Clary wasn't sure what caused one to live below their potential. In essence, it had more to do with the mind giving up on whatever was happening around them. People tended to be oblivious to the energy, and very few recognized it. It was hard to get somebody to believe in the miracles. It was easy to give up when people couldn't think beyond the ordinary and had no will to survive a scenario in their own minds.

They knew nothing of what could be.

But, in Brody's case, he was an active life force, struggling to do more, to be more. He held on to life and savored it in his own way. It was fascinating and strange to get her mind wrapped around it because he was so all over the place and so alive that she felt like she was falling behind.

When you know someone to be fragile, and yet they surprise you with the strength they show, it was remarkable. It was a very strange position for her to be in. Normally she was the one in control, calmly directing energy to heal her patients.

In his case, he was jumping forward and taking the control away from her. And he wanted to do so much more already. From the moment he woke up from his coma, he considered himself ready to take on more than she had ever imagined.

She would have to up her game, do more.

She realized it now, and it was difficult for her to admit to herself. This was a strange place she was in. But it was also fascinating, and, just like her sister, Clary found herself wanting more. They always talked about it, and they knew what they could do was not enough. They wanted to grow, to learn more, and to do more.

Now that Clary had finally found a group of people who she could try to match pace with, she had become uncertain of herself. There was likely to be no end to the growth for both Cara and Clary, if they stayed here, as they had the chance to expand their abilities beyond their wildest dreams, all because they were among other people who had energy abilities.

A group of like-minded people who could wield energy would accelerate each other's growth when working together. Much faster than any others left alone. Some of them could be irritating and headstrong—Brody in particular—and she knew the risks and the trouble she would have in controlling him.

He was a force to be reckoned with, and, if the attacks on the team kept continuing, she wasn't sure how that would go down with him—or with anybody else in the group.

Her first responsibility was to keep Brody alive, but, as he said, there would be times where the conflicting goals could hinder her work. He didn't want her shutting him down when he knew he had to do something, and she couldn't, with good conscience, let him be. Before all this, her patients knew nothing of the abilities and the energy she was sustaining them with, but Brody knew. He understood, and he was fighting for control.

There had to be a level of compromise with Brody that she hadn't expected, and that was both incredibly tantalizing and appealing. She understood the draw for her sister, but, more than that, Clary had also felt the emotions that surged through her with her connection to Brody.

She was afraid that the same emotions and the same connection were deeply seated within Brody. Was it a side effect of the energy work they did? Would it happen with everybody? That was the part that concerned Clary the most. She didn't know if it was something that could only happen with a special someone.

She didn't want to think, if her sister went off and worked with another group or another person, that Cara would end up having intense feelings for someone else.

Would her connection with a future patient compromise her connection with her partner, Rick?

Clary couldn't imagine that happening because something was very special about the two of them together. Maybe it was just timing, maybe it was the depth that they'd had to go. As Clary sat pondering this, her sister nudged her gently.

"Penny for your thoughts." Cara looked worried. "You're thinking awfully loud."

Clary chuckled. "I'm thinking about the strange events that brought us here," she murmured, feeling a bit lost and scared. "Where do we go from here, and what effect does this have on the type of work we do?"

Her sister nodded in understanding. "That is something I have contemplated quite a bit lately myself," she murmured, "and, like you, at the moment, there's no clear-cut answer."

"No, there isn't, is there?" Clary was exhausted, as she stared at the group working around them. "So many energy-working people are here. It feels odd."

"Well, it might feel odd. Yet, at the same time, it also feels …" Cara stopped and murmured, "right somehow."

Clary looked at her and nodded. "I can feel that. You feel it's right, but you've had the time to come to terms with it. For me, it's brand new," she admitted, "so that rightness isn't there yet."

"And I get that too." Cara gave her a gentle smile. "It's an interesting conundrum we're up against."

"It is, and not exactly something I'd expected, when you called on me."

"No, but we never really know from one day to the next, from one job to the next. When we do get called and see what we're up against, our responses are all in the moment."

"I know, and I was thinking about that. I need your opinion. Like, if you do another job, and you have to go this deep again, do you lose the connection you already have?" She pointed out Rick, the man she was speaking about. "Or can you just not go as deep anymore? Or can you go as deep and no longer have the same problem? Maybe once you connect like this, you don't have this same depth of connection available to you?"

Cara replied thoughtfully, "Believe me. That is something that I've thought about because our work is important. It's really important to me to continue doing this, and I was wondering that too. I won't know until the moment presents itself again."

"Right, but I need some confirmation." Clary sounded desperate.

"I'm wondering if this would act as a ground for us," Cara murmured.

She stared at her sister in surprise. "So you're saying that Brody could become a ground for me?"

"I don't know," Cara murmured, as she turned to look at Brody, who was deep in conversation with the others. "When you think about it, we have crossed into uncharted territory, and maybe"—she shrugged with a half smile—"maybe we get to determine what they become to us."

Stumped, Clary stared at her sister, wondering at the depth of that realization. "You mean, we have a choice?" she asked in a surprised tone.

"It is something that we have often wondered about and have only had the choice in terms of who we thought could be helped and who couldn't. Then, once committed, we didn't really have much choice."

"Exactly," Clary agreed. "And again, like I said, this is all relatively new, but what if we made it something that we could choose? What if we decided based on how it would affect us?"

"But that is too messy. I don't want that," Cara argued against her sister's thought process. "The whole idea was to have this be something that determines how we help others, not to leech off our emotions."

"No, absolutely not," Clary stated in full agreement. "We have to make the decisions that we need to make and to know that everybody around us will be safe and not affected by our energy—whether up or down. That includes new patients."

"Exactly," Cara murmured.

At that, Terk entered the room and saw the two women standing together. A smile played on his face.

Clary murmured to Cara, "It's almost like he's a magnet for troubled energy."

"I think he is in some ways." Cara laughed.

Terk immediately headed to them, drawing attention from everybody else around. As he stopped in front of them, he said. "It's really not that bad."

Immediately Clary laughed. "That's what we were just discussing, trying to figure out what this means to us."

"Well, hopefully it'll mean all good things," Terk stated, "but, either way, believe me. You have my gratitude for everything you've done so far."

Clary nodded gently. "And, as you and I both know, gratitude means jack shit when it comes to dealing with the next person."

He burst out laughing. "You're very honest, and I really appreciate that. For the record, I think you're worrying over nothing."

"Yeah, it's not your heart and soul engaged," Clary shared. "It's something that we do have to consider. Our work is very important to us."

"We do want to continue doing it," Cara pitched in.

"I'm glad to hear that," Terk replied. "A lot of people out there need your particular brand of care."

At that, Brody walked over and obviously had been listening in on part of the conversation. "I know that I'm part of the problem, so, if there's anything I can do to ease it up, please let me know."

Clary shook her head. "Not until you're healed."

"And here I thought I was doing so much better," he said, with a bit of a wry tone.

"You are," Clary confirmed immediately. "Absolutely you are. But you are not out of danger yet."

Stumped, he stared at her. "I'm walking. I'm talking, and I can use energy again. What kind of danger could there possibly be?"

At that, she turned and looked at Terk. "I gather they haven't seen the pitfalls. Have they?"

Terk immediately shook his head. "No, in all of our training, I've been very careful to keep things flowing smoothly."

"You can't always keep everything flowing smoothly," Clary argued. "Particularly when it comes to this kind of energy work."

At that, the others gathered around.

"Hang on a minute. … Are you saying there's something we don't know about?" Damon asked.

Terk smiled. "Clary's bringing up an issue that, at some point in time, we would get to. I have hinted at it many

times, but it goes along with the need to not be overconfi-
dent with energy and to realize that there will always be
somebody or something out there who can do more. More
than what I or you can do. These two women are prime
examples. I called on them to help because I knew their
abilities went way beyond anything that we've seen before,
and I knew that they had that ability to reach out and to help
each one of you."

Everyone was listening in by now.

"Obviously we all owe them a tremendous amount of
thanks." Terk continued to make his point. "However, that's
not what they are looking for. They're looking for an ability
to move on themselves, wholly and completely, so they can
potentially become stronger."

At that, Rick walked over, placed a hand on Cara's
shoulder. "Hopefully moving on doesn't mean moving out,"
he muttered.

Everybody heard the worry in his voice.

"Not at all," Cara stated immediately. "But, as you
know, my work is important to me."

He nodded, slowly sensing there was a *but* coming.

"But, … like I mentioned earlier, our work is as important to us as your abilities are to you. So keeping them
functioning and flowing is critical," Clary added.

"Does any of that have something to do with me?" Brody asked, staring at her.

"No," she replied. "In many ways, you've enhanced it.
But that enhancing in itself is a problem." It was obvious he
didn't like her answer.

He sat down with a *thump*. "I can see this brings up
something that I never expected."

"Neither did I," she stated calmly. "Does that mean I

regret it? No, of course not. Your life is important, and the fact that you can also work energy means I can see even more value in saving you."

"But not to the detriment of yourself," he exclaimed.

"And I don't think it has been a detriment to myself," she murmured. "However, I do think that we have entered uncharted territory, and none of us knows what we're facing."

"Agreed," Terk stated. "Yet, at the same time, I find it fascinating."

"Sure." Clary gave him a wry look. "You're not the guinea pig."

Startled, he looked at her and then burst out laughing again.

"I do like to hear your laughter," Clary noted wistfully. "You don't do it much."

He stopped, staring at her. "And how do you know that?" he asked.

She looked at him in amazement. "The same way you knew to call us to help your team. I can sense it. I can feel it." She looked over at Cara for confirmation, and Cara immediately nodded.

"Absolutely," Cara agreed. "There is only so much that we can't see. And we're not trying to see in the sense of … I mean to say that we're not trying to interfere or, you know, cross the privacy line," she explained. "But there are some things that are pretty hard for us *not* to see. And that would be emotional health as well as physical health, for one example."

Terk nodded slowly. "Fascinating thought."

Clary shrugged. "Maybe, but, at the same time, an awful lot is going on here that none of us has been exposed to, so it'll take some cooperation to work through it."

Brody looked at Cara, then over at Rick. "If I am not mistaken, it will take the two of you to work through it. I hope it's not a misunderstanding on my part, but are you suggesting that Clary and I do the same?"

Rick immediately nodded. "We have worked through a lot, and we're looking forward to working through the rest," he stated. "There is a connection between us that is deeper than I had ever thought was possible," he murmured. "And, for that, I'm grateful."

"So," Clary explained, "the question that I had brought up to my sister was that, if we connect with the next dying person, and we go this deep with that next patient, will we have the same connection? And would it diminish the prior connection, like the one Cara has built right now with Rick?" Clary finally broached the one subject she knew that nobody was willing to really look at.

At that, Rick gasped, and he stared at Clary, then Cara in horror.

Clary shrugged. "It is something that needs to be discussed."

"I hadn't necessarily thought to bring it up so publicly though," Cara noted, with a wry tone.

"There is no privacy when it comes to this," Clary murmured. "So I'm sorry if we're crossing lines or opening up things that you wanted to keep private, but I think it's more important that we all examine things and be aware of the fact that there could be changes that affect the whole team."

"Changes?" Rick murmured, as he stared at Clary.

At that, Brody sat down right beside her. "Is that what you're expecting to happen with us?"

"I don't know what I'm expecting to happen with us,"

Clary stated. "But, if you tell me that there's no bond between us, I'll call you a liar flat-out."

He looked at her, startled. "Well, that's clear."

She shrugged. "I don't really have the time or energy to waste on any mind games," she declared. "I think at some point it is bound to happen, and everybody should know, given what you have all have gone through together. You and I are connected at a level that I don't think either one of us expected."

Brody nodded slowly. "That's fair. And I'm seeing that kind of connection slowly build in the other couples around us. Is that not true?" he asked Damon and Tasha in particular.

Slowly Tasha nodded. "It's not what I expected because I was always at ground zero. Before this, there was a possibility that something would deepen our relationship, but no doubt that our situation has definitely pushed the limits of our relationship."

"I don't think you're correct there," Clary disagreed. "I think you've just opened up the door. I don't think you've hit the limit at all."

Tasha looked at her in surprise. "You know what? I wouldn't be against that. Damon has been part of my heart for a very long time, and to have him reside in my heart is nothing more than what I would expect."

At that, Clary smiled gently. "And because that bond was always there, I think it's made the connection between you two even easier," she murmured. "You didn't have to start from the beginning because you already had that connection there, so the energy could flow faster and smoother, as soon as you allowed it to." She looked over at Damon and nodded. "And I can see on your face that the connection was there for you as well."

He nodded. "I was one of those guys who thought I should not get involved with her because it would affect our working relationship, and our work was very important." He paused. "I kind of always thought it would be a *later* thing."

"And then later happened when you weren't looking?" Clary asked, with a smile.

He gave her a wry look. "Later happened, and I thought we were done for when this team was disbanded, then attacked." He waved an arm around. "But I was wrong. It's a bond that I had hoped for, had dreamed about, but never really expected to ever see."

"Well, that's good news then," Clary noted, "because your relationship is obviously getting stronger and stronger, and I can see that it will continue to do so."

At that, Tasha slipped her hand into Damon's and nodded.

Clary looked over at Sophia and asked, "What about you?"

"We'd had a thing, then he stood me up, but there's no doubt that we have always had a connection. I came as soon as Terk called because I hadn't been ready to walk away from Wade," she murmured. "I don't think it's the same as what you guys have, but our connection is growing constantly."

At that, Wade walked over and wrapped an arm around her shoulders to hold her close. "And I've certainly felt that myself," he muttered. "I'm really glad you brought this up," he said, looking at Clary. "I hadn't really considered that this was something everybody was going through. And maybe, in a way, I'm not too happy about it either," he admitted, with a wry smile, "because I guess I was thinking it was special for just the two of us."

Sophia looked up at him and nodded. "Me too."

"It is special, in that it's just about the two of you," Cara noted. "Nobody here feels exactly the same way as you do, but, if we all understand it rightly, each pair here has a deeper connection than they had ever expected. You have to realize that a lot of this is because of the energy that you're utilizing. The more energy that moves around and through you, then the more energy you use and, thus, with more usage, the more your abilities grow. This is good, as it will help keep all of us safe as we move forward."

"So you're thinking that this special energy connection will be necessary for whatever lies ahead?" Wade asked.

Clary nodded. "I would expect it to be that way with all of you, whether you have acknowledged a special connection or not," she noted, looking over at Mariana.

"It's the reason I came," Mariana admitted. "I knew Cal was in trouble first and foremost. And then Terk contacted me with the news that Cal was injured." She nodded. "He had insisted we be apart so that our son would be safe, but, in the end, we were both kidnapped, so finally Cal's been convinced that we are stronger and safer together than we can ever be apart."

"And you see how that's the kind of bond that, once it already exists, you can really build on," Clary added. "So you're all very blessed, and I hope you understand just how special what you are sharing is."

The couples nodded.

"I sure hope so," Gage stated. "It's been the same story with me and Lorelei."

"What about you?" Rick asked, looking over at Brody. "Is it the same for you?"

Brody shrugged it off, looking over at Clary.

"Well, let's just say that we're still working on that connection," Clary replied. "I haven't been the most open about it because, as far as I'm concerned, he's still my patient."

At her side, Brody whispered, "Ouch."

But, of course, everybody heard.

She smiled at him. "And that blunt frankness is what you would expect from me too," she noted. "As much as you want me to declare you healed and cut you loose, you also don't want me to leave."

BRODY CRINGED. HAVING her speak so openly in front of everybody was a little bit like having a part of his shield ripped down, leaving him exposed. It was uncomfortable, and Brody thought she knew it, but it didn't matter because, to her, this was important to share with everyone in the room.

Looking at her, he said, "I don't really know what I feel. I've always kept myself quite isolated and alone. Mostly because of the type of work we do. It's like Damon said. We didn't want to bring anybody else in to get hurt."

"Of course not. I understand," Clary murmured, as she studied him.

Something was almost magnetic about her gaze, and he didn't understand it, but this compulsion to talk to her was something he'd never felt before. He looked over at Terk. "Did you know any of this would happen?"

"No." Terk studied them all with an odd look. "But I find it fascinating that it's happening with all of you."

"But then, if you think about it," Cara noted, "every level has been affected. Every one of these people has gone through their own personal Waterloo and personal epiphany of what's important in life, then chosen somebody they want to be with for the rest of their days."

"However long that should be," Brody muttered.

"The fact that you say it that way is a little painful, but it doesn't need to be," Clary stated immediately. "I'm stating the truth."

"And I find that fascinating too," Damon added, "because these are truths that we wouldn't normally talk about."

At that, Cara immediately smiled and nodded. "Of course not. Everybody on Terk's team likes to keep their emotions at bay and private. But understand that, in our world, there is no privacy because we can see so much in the energy around you. We see what is going on with each and every one of you, and we can't deal in anything but truth."

"In all honesty, it does affect us to the core," Clary shared, true to her sister's point. "So, once that connection is made, you guys need to understand that your thoughts and actions will affect everybody around you as well."

"Is that a good thing or a bad thing?" Sophia asked.

"For me, it's a good thing," Cara stated. "You don't have to worry about where you stand or wonder what somebody else is thinking. You don't have to worry about what somebody will say when you do something that is for you but not necessarily for both of you," she murmured. "If that makes any sense."

"Well, it does, … and it doesn't." Sophia laughed. "But I can see what you mean."

"There is that …" Clary stopped, looking for the words. "What I meant to say is, there's a sense of … security. There is that security, that inner knowing that whatever is happening is happening for the right reason, and you can go with it.

You can go with that flow and experience a level of bonding that I had never imagined we could have."

"You also have to understand that these men share that bond already, being Terk's team," Cara murmured.

Terk immediately nodded. "That's very true. That bond is a major part of why we're so effective as a team. We are connected, and everybody's well-being is important to us. What we have done is expanded that bonding beyond the team to include the new additions to the family."

Brody felt something inside him shrinking a little bit because they were all talking as if he and Clary were a couple, and they weren't. He wasn't even sure how any of that worked, but he and Clary certainly hadn't gotten to that point, and he wasn't sure that was something they would get to.

How could they?

He wasn't sure how to handle it in this public setting either. Thankfully nobody seemed to be pushing and probing at their relationship, and soon he felt a sense of relief about maybe having some space to think this through. A sense of fatigue hit him, and he frowned at that. He looked over at her. "Are you knocking me out by any chance?"

She looked at him in surprise. "Nope, that's not for me to do." She studied him. "But you're definitely getting tired, so maybe you should go rest."

He shrugged. "Maybe I should, but, at the same time, it's really not where I want to be."

"Did you just ask if she was knocking you out?" Tasha asked in surprise. "Can you feel that?"

"I felt my energy draining," he noted. "And I have to admit that this is all so new and very confusing on my side. Plus I'm still not back to normal, so honestly some of this conversation is uncomfortable."

"Of course it is," Cara agreed immediately. "And you haven't had much time at all to heal."

He shrugged. "It feels like I've healed, but I can see that, from some perspectives, maybe not as much as I thought."

"Definitely not as much as you would like to think," Clary replied gently. "And rest is something you need to do to get there."

He nodded. "I'm still not sure why it hit me all of a sudden." He looked over at Clary suspiciously.

She snorted. "Go deal with your own problems. I didn't knock out your energy."

"So, what happened then?"

"I removed *my* energy, and just … separated," she said succinctly. At the same time, she got up, glaring at him. "And you're welcome." With that, she turned and walked out.

Brody was looking at Terk, questioning the validity of the answer he just got. "Seriously?"

"I'm not sure." Terk looked at him quietly. "But, if she says so, I would tend to believe her."

He snorted. "Well, that would be easier said than done, considering that she just walked out on me."

"Well, you did accuse her of doing something underhanded," Terk noted, looking at him sharply.

Brody winced at that. "I didn't mean it that way. It's just, all of a sudden, I'm exhausted, and the bed seems a very long way from here."

Cara smiled. "Maybe she did it to prove a point. But the fact of the matter is, you haven't really understood how involved she has been in keeping you moving, and now that she's tired and needs a break, she removed her energy from you to reenergize herself, and you're dropping."

"But that would mean she was using so much of her energy in order to keep me functioning," Brody suggested, "and I didn't even think that was possible." He now looked at her suspiciously.

"Not only is it possible, it's true," Cara noted calmly. "I've seen her energy moving through your system at a constant rate. She regulates what you're burning and what you're not because you still haven't got a handle on it yourself. In theory, you should be in bed resting, but, because you insist on walking around, poking your nose in everything, you are draining both yourself and Clary. What you really need is bed rest."

He could see it now.

Cara continued. "She has had to step away more for your sake than hers, what with believing it was just you doing this. Maybe Clary is letting you get used to the after effects of your day. You don't understand just how weak you are, so she has removed her energy to show you." Cara suddenly stopped and looked at him, frowning. "No, she hasn't removed it completely. More like slowed down the flow to you so that she can go rest herself and so that you have a chance to experience what it feels like to function on your own."

And, with that, Cara got up. "Honestly I'm kind of tired too. So I'll go crash myself." She smiled at the others. "I'll see you in a little bit." And she started to walk out.

Immediately Rick rushed to her side, and together they left.

Brody looked over at Terk. "Good God, I hate to ask, but I'm not even sure I'll make it to the bed."

At that, Terk nodded. "And that's likely why Clary did

it. Were you by any chance thinking that she should maybe leave already and that you didn't need her?"

He winced. "Of course I was. Besides, it's not like we're a couple. You know for a fact that I don't do relationships well. It's a nightmare come true. Here all you guys have this incredible bond with somebody, and she supposedly has the same bond with me. Not to mention that I don't even know her. Of course it's uncomfortable. And maybe I didn't like the public discussions either."

Terk immediately nodded. "It was an interesting conversation though," he murmured. "And to see that those two women can do so much is just fascinating."

Brody got up, then shook his head. "I need to go lie down." He frowned, looked at Terk, and whispered, "Help me?"

"Sure, and you also have something else to do as well. So you better think on it."

"Oh, *great*. Now I have some thinking to do." He took two steps, and the floor reached up to hit him in the face.

CHAPTER 9

BRODY'D BEEN OUT for the last four hours, as Clary sat by his bedside, wondering about keeping him under for more time but figured he would probably just be even more pissed.

When the door opened, and Terk walked in, he raised an eyebrow and whispered, "How is he doing?"

"Healing," Clary replied shortly. "Although he's definitely trying to find his way out. He is restless and trying to resurface." Terk frowned at that, and she confirmed what they both knew to be true. "He's stubborn, cranky, and always wants to be part of the action."

Terk looked up, and his grin flashed. "I can't really blame him for that either. Listen. I really appreciate what you're doing."

She nodded. "You do, but he doesn't."

"And that public conversation out there was intended to do what?"

"Put him on notice," she stated. "And help everybody else understand what a gift they have."

"Yet you're afraid you don't have the same gift?"

"The thing is, I really do," she noted. "I'm not sure how I'll separate from him, but I promise you, I will." She said it with more determination in her voice, even though she didn't know how to handle it. "I can't live connected but not connected fully. That's not who I am. At some point in time, he'll have to make a decision too. But this just isn't the time. He hasn't a clue whether he's coming or going yet, and I think he feels, in some way, like he's being manipulated."

Terk sucked in his breath and then slowly nodded. "I can't blame him for that. I can see how he would potentially feel that way."

"Well, you can explain it to him when he gets here," she suggested, with half a smile. "Right now he just needs to heal. I'm not keeping him under now. I was," she admitted, "but now I'm slowly letting him resurface."

"Good," Terk replied, "and I think you're right. I think he would hate to know that you had that much control over him."

"He already knows it, and he already hates it," she stated, "but that doesn't change the fact that he is incapable of being on his own yet. And, when I withdrew my energy, as I recently did, he got the first warning of it."

"I don't think he thought much of that either." Terk smiled.

"Of course not. We always like to think we're invincible. Maybe he'll be that way again, and maybe he won't, but, in the meantime, he needs to get enough energy back so that he can stand on his own two feet. That means not doing anything to overexert himself and definitely not draining energy from other people as fast as he is doing right now."

Terk looked at her sharply.

"And, yes, I can see him pulling on you too," she said. "He's a very determined person, and you've taught them well. At the same time, he needs to know his own boundaries in terms of his physical health."

"None of us like hearing that," Terk admitted, smiling.

"No, and, at some point in time"—she stared at him—"you'll drop too. Have you thought about that?"

"I have," he noted. "I'm just not quite there yet."

"You're not"—she nodded—"but that doesn't mean that your energy isn't."

He winced. "Well, hopefully you and your sister will be around to help me, if that happens."

"*When*, not if." She calmly studied him. "And chances are you'll do too much, and you'll be the one who goes down in the middle of something."

"I hope not," he said. "I do my best to not let anybody down."

"And that's the problem," she said. "It is up to you to take some time for yourself. Be yourself and let it be okay to let them down every once in a while. Right now, you need more, and you're not giving it to yourself."

"I can't yet."

She heard the resolve in his voice. "And I get that," she murmured. "I just think you're making a mistake by keeping it from them."

"But if they knew, they wouldn't continue to heal."

"Well, Cara is doing what she can for individual members, as am I, but my main focus has to be Brody," she admitted. "And he's just not easy."

Terk's lips twisted. "No, he's definitely not easy, but he's also an incredibly capable energy worker, when he's healthy."

"But he's not healthy. That's the point. He's not healthy yet, which means that, at this moment, he's not capable of anything," she muttered. "Trying to get him to understand that there are some things he has to do has been impossible so far."

Terk smiled. "Your patience and tolerance are appreciated."

She laughed. "Maybe by you, but definitely not by him."

"He will appreciate it when he fully understands," Terk stated, "but understanding also means acceptance."

"He's still fighting the reality of his situation."

Terk nodded. "And I think most of us would in that same scenario," he muttered. "None of us wants to accept being weaker than we thought we were—or less capable than we've been before. We pride ourselves on what we can do, and, I think, to some extent, right or wrong, we measure our own worth based on what we can do for the team. It has become a norm to measure ourselves against what the rest of the team is doing."

"I think that is a hardship. It's also a failing of your judgment," she announced, glaring at him. "You need to change that."

He grinned at her. "You see? Having you guys here has been really good."

"Maybe," she muttered, "but there's definitely room for some change."

"There is, indeed," he murmured. "And believe me. We see it happening even now."

"That is a good thing." She shrugged and continued. "However, it's also frustrating because you guys could do so much more that you haven't done yet."

"And the longer you're here with us," Terk noted, "the more we will learn."

"I'll help him to wake up now. I'm sure it's about time to get him up and moving. He most certainly needs some food as well," she added, "and then I'll assess where he's at."

Terk nodded. "You might want to take it a little easy on him."

She laughed. "You know what? I get that I have a really rough reputation out there," she murmured. "Yet I really do have his care in mind."

"And I know you do," Terk agreed. "Are you always quite so harsh with your patients?"

"No, not always," she said, "unless they don't behave, and then, well, all bets are off."

At that, Terk nodded. "We're preparing a meal now, so how long do you think it'll take him?"

"I'd say give him ten, fifteen, or maybe even twenty minutes," she replied. "He's just starting to pull out of it now."

And, with that, Terk left.

Clary waited until Brody opened his eyes. He frowned when he saw her, and, unable to help it, she frowned right back.

"What happened?" he asked.

"You stood and collapsed," she stated succinctly.

He stared at her. "I can't remember the last time I collapsed, … if ever."

He frowned, probably wondering about her involvement in this embarrassment or whether she could have made it up.

She sighed. "No, you probably can't remember it happening before, but this time it did. Whether you like it or not, that's what happened. Now that you're awake and obviously a whole lot more cognizant than you were before, I'll leave you to get up, to get dressed, and to join us all. They're preparing a meal, and you need to get out there and join everyone."

"And if I don't?" he asked, a note of challenge in his voice.

She looked at him and stated calmly, "Well then,

your … recovery … will … take … even … longer." She chewed on each word, taking time to spit each one out. "Your choice." With that, she walked out.

She had to wonder why she was banging her head against the wall. This man was not in any way someone she ever would have chosen for herself. She was still pondering that when she walked into the kitchen, and there was her sister, sitting with Rick.

Clary walked over and wrapped her arm around Cara. The hugs were their thing, and they had a calming effect. Clary had learned that a long time ago.

Immediately her sister hopped up and wrapped her up in her arms. "Pretty rough?"

Clary just shrugged and didn't say anything. Obviously a lot of people were around, and privacy was at a premium. "It'll be fine," she whispered to her. "He's awake and should be hungry, if and when he can get himself up." She walked over to pour herself a cup of coffee.

"I don't think anybody has thanked you," Damon noted. "Love him, but Brody is not an easy person."

She looked at him and raised an eyebrow. "That's an understatement." Then she walked over and sat down beside her sister.

Mariana was in the kitchen, and it looked as if she was enjoying every minute of it.

Deciding that she needed something to keep her busy, Clary walked over, and spoke up, kind of wondering out loud. "I don't know how you do it." Mariana was a force to be reckoned with, and they all appreciated it. "You're here cooking the whole time. I would go nuts."

"And yet I love it," Mariana said, with a smile.

"Is there something I can do to help?" Clary asked, in a

tone that sounded more like, *I could use something to keep my mind busy.*

Mariana looked at her closely and then nodded. "Absolutely. A little bit of help here and there is nice. I've got potatoes over there. If you want, you can mash them."

"I think I can manage that." And that's where Clary was when Brody walked in, tired and definitely looking like he was not up to par.

He stepped inside the kitchen, and the others looked up.

"There you are," Tasha said gently. "How are you doing now?"

"Well, better than I was." He restlessly looked around, and, when his gaze landed on Clary, he immediately seemed to settle. "I hadn't realized how bad it was," he admitted. "Until I stood up and then *boom*. I guess I just collapsed."

"You did," Tasha agreed. "As long as you're okay now?"

"I'm fine," he told her. "I just have to remember that my energy is not where I thought it was."

"Maybe that's because it wasn't all your energy," Cara noted.

"Apparently," he replied, his tone turning brisk. "Something else that needs to be remedied."

Clary knew there wasn't anything anybody could say to that. It was obviously a problem, and yet no one could take care of it. It had to be him—and him alone. He wouldn't tolerate being weak for much longer. At the same time, while he didn't have the strength to do anything about it, he needed whatever Clary could give him.

He walked over sat down close to where Clary was, as if it were the most natural thing in the world.

She didn't say anything to him, as she finished her potato mashing and then turned to Mariana. "What else can I do?" Without question, Mariana put her on setting the table. When she had that done, she went back for more chores.

Just keeping busy was keeping her sane. And anything was better than sitting beside Brody, realizing that he was just trying to get rid of her. Some things were harder to deal with than others. She'd had cranky patients, and she'd had patients who healed really well. And, as soon as they thought that they were doing well enough, they wanted to get rid of her, fast.

She typically was gone as soon as she could, but there were also times when she'd had to go to the people who had hired her to explain that the patient wasn't quite ready. She'd never had an argument from any of the patients themselves. She knew they could be difficult, cranky, and miserable. But she hadn't ever come across one who was quite so determined to be as independent as Brody was. It was an interesting circumstance to find herself in—and not one she was particularly enjoying.

BRODY WAS SHAKEN by the awareness of just how weak he'd become.

Of course he needed to wrap his mind around the fact that it wasn't that he'd become that weak but that he'd remained weak, ever since the initial attack on the team and the subsequent coma. He just thought he was doing so much better; yet all that energy in him was coming from her.

It was due to Clary.

He was mad at himself for having become so weak. He needed to do something about it. But what?

He'd been attacked and in a coma for weeks, and, only

just now, he saw his body failing to the extent that he realized just how much he needed her, now more than ever.

And how damn ungrateful he'd been.

That was a sobering reality. He had never really considered himself an asshole, until now.

Well, this was something that he needed to fix, but it was hard to do anything when it was so obvious and so public. Not exactly the way he wanted to function in life, and she would probably be the first to point it out.

It didn't matter that he wanted to make it right. Life happened, and he would just deal with it. The trouble was, apparently he *wasn't* dealing with it.

Another sobering reality.

Still, he was here, and he would get food because he needed it. He had decided earlier that he would do whatever kind of therapy was needed to fix this. And he would have to ask her for help.

So be it.

He had never really considered himself somebody so incapable of asking for help that, even when it was obviously something he needed, he couldn't ask for it. All throughout the meal he stayed quiet, but he ate generously and enough to fuel himself well.

Trying to register where his own health markers were, he needed a handle on his own energy markers too. When he was full, he stopped to reassess, and only then did he put down his fork. Nobody said anything to him, but the chatter around him continued in a regular swell of varying conversations.

He was brought out of his thoughts only when Terk and Damon started talking about their plans. The plan was the trigger that perked him up. "Have you made plans?" Brody asked, trying to hold back a building resentment that he'd been kept out of it.

"No," Terk replied, immediately putting Brody back into the loop. "But the tracks around our perimeter are getting stronger."

"So, they know where we are?"

"They just haven't found a way to breach our defenses."

After a moment's pause, Clary looked over at Terk. "So, we have an imminent attack, I presume?"

"Do you feel it too?" Terk asked.

She nodded. "I do, though I wasn't sure what I was feeling. Thanks for the clarification." That's all she said.

Brody was kind of stunned at that. She was taking this calmly.

Moments later, she spoke again. "Are we making plans for countering it?" she asked cautiously.

"Of course." Terk looked at her. "Some. … Well, it is a work in progress. Merk, my brother, is on his way, and we've got surveillance set up outside," Terk added. "The bottom line is that, as soon as there's any kind of warning, I'm hoping that you, Brody, and Cara can set up a shield for everybody."

"We can do that," Brody replied, knowing he wasn't up for it, but, with her help, it was possible. "Of course I was hoping to do a little more than just set up a shield."

"At this point in time, a shield is the most important thing you could possibly do. Nothing more important," Wade stated.

"I gather that an awful lot changed in your world, Brody, but that camouflage is something that none of us can do," Gage noted.

At that, Brody agreed. "I can see that."

"An awful lot of extra people are here with us now, and we don't want anybody hurt," Calum added.

"No. Of course not," Brody stated, more surprised than anything. "I'm fine with that. Do I get a little warning though? I'm not …" Then he stopped, a bit unsure of himself. He needed to tell them, and he winced at the thought of having to admit it out loud. Swallowing his pride, he explained, "I'm not as healed as I had hoped I was."

He felt Clary looking at him. Every chance he'd gotten to sit beside her, she'd got up and moved, but somehow he managed to finagle it again. When he sat down for the meal, she was right beside him. She hadn't looked at him and had deliberately avoided him.

He couldn't blame her though. He'd been an ass to her, which was not something he was terribly proud of, but the damage had already been done.

"I think it's very important that you recognize that," Terk noted. "A lot is going on. More than we can possibly handle and manage individually. It has to be a team opera-tion. You cannot go rogue on this one."

"We'll do what we can, when we can," all the team members confirmed to Terk.

"Brody, if you can handle a camouflage to keep the women and the little guy protected," Terk noted, "I would take that as being the most important thing you could possibly do."

Brody nodded. "I agree. Obviously I'm still adjusting, still healing, but hopefully, by then, I will be back up on my feet."

"You don't have very long," Terk shared. "So I suggest, after you're done eating, you might want to go lie down for as long as you can."

He stared at them, then winced. "Will do, but only if Clary can bring me out when I am needed."

Clary remained silent, but Terk intervened. "Absolutely. We'll need you."

"I will," Clary reassured Brody, "but you need to rest, so you'll be as strong and as fit as possible."

"We probably should have left you at the apartment, but hindsight and all that," Terk admitted.

"You didn't have the manpower to leave me where I was," Brody said, being brutally honest. "And you knew it. Much better to have me here, where I could at least contribute somewhat."

"We need more than *somewhat*," Damon noted, his tone hard. "Everything we care about is in this room," he murmured. "Nothing is more important to us than making sure they all get through this."

Brody agreed. "I have no problem with that." He looked over to see Little Calum staring at him with an odd look on his face.

"Does anybody recognize the fact that Little Calum here has more insights than a lot of us?" Brody asked.

Mariana looked at her son proudly. "I've seen that too. I'm surprised you have though."

Calum nodded. "I noticed too, but I haven't had a chance to mention it to Mariana."

She stared at him in shock, then looked at Little Calum. "Is that what he's doing right now? His focus is all over the place."

"It is, and so is his energy," Calum added. "Apparently some of the blood runs true."

"*All* of the blood runs true," Cara corrected. "It's just a matter of how strong his abilities are."

Right on cue, Little Calum spoke up. "Men," he said in excitement. "There are men outside."

Terk looked at him and nodded. "They are, aren't they?" he murmured, as he looked over at the others. "Not inside yet," he murmured, "but another visit."

"Just a recon." Damon hopped up and headed toward the rear door.

"Yes, but much more intense, and they're using some kind of technology to see who and what is in here," Wade said.

Immediately Brody felt an attack on his senses. He instinctively sent up a shield surrounding the entire group.

Terk looked over at him and nodded. "Just remember to conserve your energy."

"I can sense that this is not the main attack," Brody told them.

"This will be something else," Terk confirmed. "I think more along the lines of trying to sort out where we are and how to get in," he muttered.

"But we can't take the chance of your being wrong either," Brody noted.

"No, we sure can't," Terk murmured. "So, if you've got something to add, please do so."

Brody frowned at that. "I'm done eating, so I'll go and set up a camouflage on the building itself." And, with that, he turned and walked away. Almost immediately he sensed somebody beside him and realized that—for all his previous efforts to stay separate, which ended earlier today—Clary was now in the face of danger and right beside him. "It's probably not a good idea to have you with me."

"Yeah, probably not," she agreed, "but what the hell? … It seems like there's no point in arguing about it right now.

We need to fend this off together."

He looked over at her in surprise. "Does that mean you won't shut me down?"

"I haven't shut you down yet," she corrected. "Don't give me a reason to, and I won't have to."

He frowned at that. "So I guess taking away my energy doesn't constitute the same thing to you?" he asked curiously, as they walked through to the computer room, then on toward the bedrooms.

"Absolutely not," she snapped, "because I didn't take away *your* energy. All I did was take away *my* energy. I just separated myself."

He nodded. "So you said before. I just didn't realize how much of your energy it took to keep me functioning."

"Of course you didn't. You're stubborn." She said it in such a way that there was no judgment, more like just stating a fact.

He burst out laughing. "Well, I guess I should be grateful for small mercies that you kept me going this long."

"Yes, you should," she replied, emphasizing every word. "Gratitude doesn't appear to be part of your makeup." She was staring him down now.

He frowned at that. "Wow. That was a direct hit."

"Not even close," she said, "but you have a lot more of those coming."

He looked at her sharply. "Have I been such an asshole that I deserve it?"

"Not at all, just … stubborn. And because you're stubborn and obnoxious, you're not doing as well as you could be."

He groaned. "It's been a shock to realize that I wasn't doing nearly as well as I thought," he admitted. "And your separating action was a very effective lesson that I'm very sorry I had to learn the hard way. Look. I've never relied on anyone else but me. I didn't wait because I was really hoping I was doing better."

"You're doing pretty amazing," she noted, "but you don't have a whole lot of room for anyone else in your life. That is making it a lot harder for you to absorb energy efficiently. You are wasting too much energy by stressing over things that aren't important."

She needed him to understand the ramifications. "When you're upset, you block me out, so we have to find other ways to get that energy into your system, which is making me work harder. It makes it more difficult on me than it should be."

He stopped outside his bedroom. "Seriously?"

She nodded. "Yes, seriously! Because you're so determined to keep me out, you're inadvertently blocking the energy that you desperately need." She shook her head. "Like I said, you're stubborn. But I've been dealing with stubborn and cranky patients for a long time. So, as much as you're trying to be unique and different, the first at the forefront," she quipped, "you're really not."

And, with that, she opened up the door to his bedroom and looked back at him.

"Shall we?"

CHAPTER 10

C LARY WALKED INTO his bedroom beside Brody and sat down on the bed. She patted the mattress and motioned for him to lie down.

Brody remained at the doorway and frowned. "If that was an invitation, it looks totally out of place for you."

She ignored that last statement. "You better crash."

"And if I can't?" he asked in frustration, wondering what she was up to.

"I'll show you a couple methods," she replied. "We have an attack coming, and you need as many defenses available as possible."

Immediately he walked over to her. "If you got any tricks to make this easier on all of us, I'm listening."

"I know Cara has already shared some of these things with Rick," Clary noted, "so I want to make sure that you're up to speed on this as well."

"Will you keep feeding me energy?" he asked. "Because obviously I can't do it on my own, not enough to maintain the camouflage we'll need for all these people."

He had admitted it before, but this time there was only sad acceptance in his voice. She looked at him and smiled. "You know you're doing fabulously well for a guy fresh out of a coma, right?"

"Seriously?" He looked at her in surprise.

"Hardly." She chuckled. "You are frustrated because you expect to be doing better, and it's just not always that way. Part of it is you're upset because everybody else was up and about before you, but you can't look at it like that. So much in life is different and unique, including the way you all were attacked and the way you've all recovered. It takes training, and it takes practice to recover from these energy attacks. In your case, day one of coming out of that coma, you are already kicking butt and taking no prisoners," she murmured. "So I really wouldn't expect more out of you than you're already doing. It's amazing that you're doing as well as you are."

He just stared at her. "That's the first time you've ever said anything like that."

"Yeah? I forget about the fragile male ego," she said, with a laugh.

He grinned because no rancor was in her voice.

"Still," she added, "it's important that we do get a couple things clear. Come here."

She proceeded to lead him through a series of exercises designed to help him control his energy, particularly in his weakened state. By the time they'd run through it a few times, he was much more confident.

"I'm wondering how I could have missed the memo." She just smiled at him. "You're good."

She heard his compliment but continued on point. "I know you have that shield up, and you're worried about anybody coming in after the people you love," she noted. "However, a few spots in your shield have holes." Using a visual technique, she led him through a series of exercises to increase the strength.

BY THE TIME they were done, he was amazed.

"I've never seen that technique before. That makes the shield a lot easier and much more fortified," he shared. "How come I didn't know about this earlier?"

"You'll find," she explained, "when you work with other energy workers, that you'll learn a lot of new stuff, and so will they. That's why it's really important to have other people like you around. What Cara and I can do is special, but the problem for us is that, up until now, we'd never found anybody else who could do this. In my case, I've been experimenting with energy for a very long time. You may learn something new if you can stick around and stop resisting me."

He nodded unashamedly. "I don't think Terk had any idea you guys could do anything quite this miraculous. This is an extremely efficient level of energy work."

"I think he did to some degree," she replied, smiling, "but we weren't too interested in joining the group at that point."

"That's too bad for all of us," Brody said. "We could have improved a lot faster."

She shrugged. "Some things have to happen in their own time."

Brody nodded. "Can't argue with that because Terk says that all the time."

"What I do want to make sure of," she added, "is that, when things do blow up, you are capable of handling whatever is coming."

"So how will I do that if I don't even have my energy back?" he asked in frustration.

"That's why it'll take two of us, for now at least," she said. "And I get that's not what you want to hear or even think about, but the fact of the matter is, if a fight's coming, it's not just you and me caught up in this but also my sister and that little boy out there."

"Not to mention everybody else," he noted, with a heavy sigh.

"Exactly, and until we know who and what is behind it all—"

"We won't get any final answers," he added thoughtfully.

"Yeah, but we can at least take them down and make sure that, whoever these guys are, they won't be useful anymore," she murmured. He looked at her sharply, as she nodded. "Yeah, and I have a few other skills we can use. I've never done a real-life application, but I have practiced a lot. I had really hoped I wouldn't have to resort to this," she admitted.

He stared at her with concern.

She shrugged. "I've been attacked by an energy worker once in my life and prepared my defense for this afterward, and I know it's available to use if I need to. … Thankfully I haven't had to use it before, but maybe this will be the time."

He stopped and stared at her and let out a low whistle. "I see the determination in your expression. You're talking about removing their energy, aren't you?"

She nodded ever-so-slowly. "Think about it. If somebody is trying to take away my energy, what do you think my system will do?"

"It'll fight back."

"And my energy system is pretty damn strong," she noted. "Yet I'm not saying nobody out there is stronger because that's a foolhardy way to approach life. But it is a defense mechanism that most people don't know about and have no way to come back from."

"I like it," he said.

"Maybe that's what we'll need when this all blows up." At that, she turned to look at him. "You do understand that there could be something serious like a physical blow up as well as an energy attack, right?"

He nodded. "Yeah, I just didn't know if you knew."

"I see the whole building going," she noted, "and I would do a lot to stop that."

"I would too," he muttered. "So, if you've got any ideas, I'd like to hear them."

"I've already talked to Terk about it somewhat," she explained. "And we can't protect the physical building. It's too huge. All our energy needs to go to protect the people on the inside."

"If that's possible, … yes," he agreed, "but camouflage is not protective. It only hides us."

"True, but what we can do is reverse that energy."

He stared at her in shock.

She shrugged. "It's something I've had to do a couple times."

"How will that work?"

"We reverse it in two ways. So, while you get the energy from them, you will throw all that energy up to protect the people inside. Meanwhile, we stop people from coming in." She continued. "We'll work on opening a path for them. Then, when they attempt to enter, we'll reverse it and throw them back outward."

He just shook his head. "I get that it's all energy, but I don't know how effective that will be, particularly when we're under the gun."

"That's why it not only has to be done," she replied, "but it has to be done in a well-coordinated manner. And we don't have much time, so we'll focus on that right now."

He listened as she went through a series of exercises, showing him how to take the energy in the palm of her hand and turn it outward and then bring it inside his system, so that his body could access it.

"We've done things like this before," Brody noted, "but never on a big scale."

"No," she agreed, "but now we have no option. The bigger, the better."

"And what is it you're expecting to happen? I mean, what are the repercussions?"

"If we can use everybody's energy to accomplish these two energy reversals," she said, "I expect the building to be severely damaged." He stared at her in shock, and she shrugged. "Like I said, I'm not worried about the building at the moment. I'm only worried about the inhabitants."

He grimaced. "I agree in theory, but, Jesus, if this goes down the way you describe, it would be awful. And it'll go down fast."

"I know," she stated, "and that's why I'm sticking with you fairly closely for the next little bit."

He stopped, then looking at her, he asked, "Do you know something I don't know?"

"Probably." She smiled. "I think we just demonstrated that."

He rolled his eyes. "Funny. Do you have any information on the attack that's coming?"

"For sure? No," she stated, "but that it's coming? Absolutely." She immediately seemed lost, looking around carefully, then focused on Brody again. "I would say within the next twenty-four hours, and we're out of time for trying to sort this out differently."

"So then why isn't everybody leaving?" he asked in frustration.

"I think Terk wants to bring this to a complete conclusion. He is planning to disable as many of the attackers as he can," she shared. "However, I've warned him that I don't think it will happen then."

"What do you mean?" Brody turned on the bed to look at her.

"I mean, I don't think it'll happen then. I think his twenty-four-hour time frame is wrong."

"And when do you think it'll happen?"

She stared at him for a long moment, but really she was reading the future history of something that nobody else could see. "Honestly I think it's pretty imminent."

The news blew him away. "Then we don't have time for this. Do you have any other people you can bring into this?" he asked. "Or is it just the two of you?"

"It's just the two of us," she confirmed. "And, of course, all of you guys."

He nodded. "I'm not too sure how much help any of us will be."

"That's the problem with having significant others in your life," she replied. "You worry about them. And that's why we're doing the camouflage to keep them safe and to keep your mind off that and on the enemy instead. However, you know that camouflage isn't enough."

"Not if we're talking about something on the scale you are," he murmured. "And that just terrifies me."

"A lot of people here feel the same way," she stated. "So

we have to do everything we can."

Just then a series of alarms went off.

She looked over at him, wincing. "This could be the start of it."

"It better not be," Brody stated. "No way in hell we're ready."

She nodded. "I don't think our attackers give a shit about that. Here we go."

Brody raced to the computer room to find the rest of them piling in behind him.

Immediately Tasha was on the computers, along with Sophia. "They're attaching something to the side of the building." She turned and looked at Terk. "What are the chances that is C-4?" she asked, fear in her voice.

"It's possible," Terk replied, "but I'm not thinking it is."

"What is it?"

"EMP," he said quietly, "and honestly that would be just as destructive, if not more so."

The others all stared at him, but Damon understood, as did most of the men.

Brody stared at Terk. "What are the chances of going out there and removing it?"

Damon immediately responded, "I'm already on it." He looked over at Wade and Gage, and the three of them headed out, fully armed. "We have to take them down, before they get it started."

"Then let me go," Brody murmured. "I can do camouflage." He frowned and looked over at Clary.

She immediately nodded. "Yes, he can go."

He snorted. "Thanks, Mom." But no jest was in his voice.

She just stared at him steadily. "Or not."

He glared at her and disappeared almost immediately.

Outside, Gage looked at him. "I get that you're not happy about this whole scenario, but you seem to be beyond miserable about it."

"Imagine if you had somebody who could knock out your energy and topple you without your say so," Brody stated.

"I get it," Damon replied, "but she also brought you back from the dead, and there are worse things than being here, like being caught out there by these assholes."

"I know," Brody admitted, "but it's still a hard thing to deal with."

"Cut her some slack, man," Damon said, and Gage nodded.

As soon as they exited the outer door, they moved in formation to the side door. Damon asked Tasha, "Is it clear? Can we get out there?" Even the team inside heard it all through the mics on their headsets.

"You're clear to go," she replied. "They've shifted to the other side. They're still placing devices around the building."

"Good enough," Damon said, and they headed out and had to stay close together because it was the only way Brody could maintain any kind of shield camouflaging them.

They raced forward, following Tasha's instructions, and carefully removed each of the items. Now they also had to contain them.

Calum walked out a few minutes later and joined them. He brought a special box, and they placed all the devices inside.

"Good enough," Damon said, with a nod. He looked at the box. "We need to keep these out of enemy hands."

"We will. No worries on that. And we'll test them out in

a safe place but not now. We don't have safeguards up for that."

Just then Tasha spoke. "Stop and huddle. They're heading your way. Coming up on the left and right. I think somebody noticed one of the devices they just planted was now missing, and they're onto you."

"Well, shit," Damon said. "If they want to bring on the fight right now, that's totally okay with me."

Immediately they gathered along the rear wall and waited, watching both possible sides where these guys could come from.

Tasha said, "Now."

And, with that, they bolted around the nearest sidewall, guns at the ready.

Brody was not armed.

That was something that really pissed him off, but it was his job to keep that camouflage up. Now with Calum joining them, it was a struggle. Yet the moment that thought crossed his mind, the camouflage was immediately strengthened, and Calum became part of it.

Brody took a long slow deep breath because he instinctively knew that was Clary. Not that she hadn't been there the whole time, but she probably just hadn't realized how much energy he would need. Reassessing, she had backed him up.

She was right earlier. He had been fighting her, and he needed to change his way of thinking about her. He shook his head at his own foolishness, and, as the two attackers approached, talking in low tones, they pointed out where the devices had been removed from the wall.

"What the hell?" the first guy asked. "What are they doing? Are they coming up behind us and taking everything down?"

"I wouldn't be at all surprised," the second guy said. The two men look nervously around.

"That's not part of our contract. We weren't supposed to even be here right now."

"I know," the second man agreed, "but you know they're watching us, and, if we even blink, we'll be taken down."

"How the hell does that happen?" the first guy asked. "We're IT weapons specialists, but even we aren't ready for this shit. These damn things are out of our league. We're not even military trained."

Brody realized that once again these were dupes being led to the slaughter. He whispered to Tasha, "These guys aren't the ones we're after. They were only sent in to set this up."

"Maybe we should have left some in place then," she suggested. "And find a way to nullify them."

"That's not a bad idea. I don't know though. If I can, I'll get Calum here to separate from the camouflage," Brody said.

At that, Terk stepped in, his voice calm and relaxed. "I'll tell them to put them back up on the wall, now that they've been nullified," he murmured.

"Have they been?"

"Yes," Terk confirmed, "the box is magnetic. It's taken away all their charges and is taking down the battery with an EMP pulse."

At that, Calum looked over at Brody and nodded, then quickly went around, placing the items back up on the wall, all while under cover of Brody's camouflage.

One of the dupes turned and pointed. "Wait. They couldn't have taken them off. Look!"

His partner stopped. "Jesus, how did we not see that?" And there on the wall in front of them was the device.

The other man backed away, his hands up. "Crap, I need to get out of here." He looked around. "You can place the rest of these. I'm done." And, with that, he bolted for the gate that led to the road.

Within ten steps, a bullet came out of nowhere and hit the man square in the forehead. Down he went, with the back of his head blown apart.

The second man cried out in shock, as he immediately raced over to his friend's side. Then he stopped, when he realized he would be next, and instead he turned and ran as fast as he could for the corner of the building, trying to save himself. But the second bullet rang out and caught him in the back.

Nobody in Brody's group moved. He whispered into his headset, "They've taken out both of their guys. Any chance they'll double back to make sure they're dead?" Those snipers are way too accurate for comfort, as are the drones.

"Nope," Terk replied. "They haven't so far."

"Well, hell," Brody said. "They didn't even leave anyone alive for us to interview."

"Nope, and that's been their MO from the start. The big bosses take any chance they can get to kill off their local hires," Terk explained quietly.

"You know who'll really be pissed now," Brody muttered.

"MI6," Damon said in a harsh voice. "But so are we because, once again, this didn't need to happen."

"No, it didn't, but, when dealing with whatever assholes are doing this, they've got leverage, and they're using that leverage to take out these men. Whether they had anything to do with us beforehand doesn't matter because they do now."

"Two more dupes dead." Damon shook his head. "As long as you have all the devices wiped and back up on the wall where they belong, pull back in. I'm heading to the roof to check for snipers."

"Be careful," Calum warned. "This is beyond serious now."

"I think we've got two snipers," Terk shared through their comms. "I'll join Damon on the roof."

"I agree," Brody noted. "The bullets came from different directions."

"Could be many more snipers or drones out there," Terk added. "So Brody, keep that camouflage solid, and the rest of you get your asses back inside as soon as you can." And, with that, Terk was gone.

CHAPTER 11

W HEN THE MEN all came back inside, everybody was immediately wrapped in hugs.

Clary stayed back ever-so-slightly, so she could check out how Brody was doing. But he walked over and pulled her into his arms, where he just held her. "Thanks for the energy."

"Like I said"—she smirked at him, as she pulled back reluctantly—"it's always been there."

"I'm just too stubborn to know a good thing when I see it." Brody sighed.

"Might need a few knocks over the head, I guess." She snorted.

"A few?" He grinned at that. "I've never seen anything like it. Whenever I needed energy, it was there. But today it was there with a difference. I could feel it, sense it, and utilize it immediately. I also knew it wasn't mine."

"No, it wasn't," she agreed. "It was mine, and at least you could use it. That's half the battle."

He nodded. "It's just a sad thing that it's taken me all this time to figure it out."

"You still haven't realized that fully," she stated, smiling. "And that's okay. You're on the way to understanding more, and that's huge."

"I hope so," he said, "because I feel like the slow learner

in the class, and I hate that."

She chuckled. "I don't think there are any slow learners when it comes to this. The fact that you're even on target is huge."

"Says you … because some of this is just too unbelievable."

"It's all unbelievable, but you're getting there," she said. "Be thankful for the small mercies and try not to hate yourself. Just ask for help when you need it."

"Agreed," he replied, "or at least I'll try my best."

"And that's all any of us can do." She turned to look at the rest of the group. "Now that everybody is safe, now what?" Then she realized not everyone was here. "Terk left?"

Brody nodded. "So did Calum and Rick."

"Where are they?"

"They've gone to the roof, looking for the snipers," Brody told her. "After that, we're all heading out as a unit to try and take them down."

"Well, thank God for that," Clary murmured. "Anything to avoid the scenario in my head."

"We're doing our best," he murmured.

She smiled. "Go then. He's calling you."

Brody looked at her in surprise. "And you knew that how?"

"Same wavelength, same transmitter," she replied. "I'm also a receiver. So you need to go."

With the rest pulling in quickly behind him, they raced off to follow Terk. Of all the things in life that he'd never had a problem with, it was trusting the intel that came from his friend.

NOW BRODY HAD finally found somebody else with the same type of abilities and energy-work success that he could wish for himself. Clary was right; they could learn a lot from each other. And, as long as he could get his own ego back in check, they were good.

He thought there was a huge future for all of them.

But, first of all, they had to deal with these assholes. And it had to be a permanent solution. Not just a temporary fix because these guys would be back, and, when they came back the next time, they would come back with more firepower, more weapons, and may well be weapons more deadly than anything Terk's team had seen so far.

Brody couldn't allow that to happen.

To stop these guys for good, Brody needed time. He had things to do, places to be, and stuff to learn, and, for the first time, he began to realize what that would mean. He was also interested in seeing just what that would mean. It would be different with Clary by his side.

He never expected to meet anybody here, but now that he had, it began to make sense. "Well," he muttered to himself, "you're such an idiot."

At that, Wade looked at him and smiled. "You're just starting to see the light, aren't you?"

"I am." He shook his head. As they raced upstairs to hit the roof, he admitted, "I didn't understand."

"That's alright," Damon replied. "Honestly, none of us did. Cara and Clary have opened up an incredibly different world for us, and I, for one, want to see what that world can bring," he murmured.

"So after this is over, then what?" Brody followed them up the staircase, immediately feeling his energy start to flag. He opened himself up, and the energy surged forward.

He sighed with sweet joy, feeling energy flow through his body like a fury, but that furious feeling lasted only a second. Now Brody was in control and calm—and recognized what feeling was truly in the center of it all. He had never seen it in his own world before.

But now there was no mistaking it. It was offered with love. He was just the idiot who hadn't seen it before. At that, he looked at the others and asked, "Ready?"

"Are you?" Damon asked.

Brody nodded, and they stepped out onto the roof together.

CHAPTER 12

CLARY SMILED AS she felt the change in Brody's demeanor and in his energy, when he accepted and utilized her energy. This time he did it for the joy of exploration. There was a delight in realizing someone was out there he could rely on.

Her sister was at her side, and an odd smile was on Cara's face. Clary couldn't hide her feelings if she wanted to. Knowing that Cara could read the same reactions, Clary let it go.

Clary was a reader too, and she read it right. Something was there. Maybe not as intense and not as close as the relationship shared by Cara and Rick but the same sensation of understanding what Brody was going through was shared with Clary, and she knew it was the beginning of something.

Cara looked over at Clary. "Very special," she whispered.

"Very," she agreed.

Cara patted Clary on the shoulder, got up, and added, "Enjoy the ride."

But Clary was a long way away from enjoying the ride; in fact, she was a long way away from anything along that line. She could hope that maybe she and Brody would get there.

She wasn't even sure what she wanted from him. It's just that everything had blown up in her face so fast, and, unlike him, she felt she hadn't had much choice. She'd made the decision to go down this road, and, even knowing what she now knew, she wouldn't change what she'd done. At the same time, she might have reconsidered some of her options back then.

And then she thought about it and shook her head.

No, she wouldn't have. Because the bottom line was, Brody had been desperately in need of her help. She had every right to be here with him.

Even though she hadn't expected it to be like this, she didn't think she could have pulled back. All she did was help, and right now he needed her.

He was a good person. He was always a protector, and how can you not help somebody like that?

Of course, in her world, she met all kinds of people, and lots of people didn't help others in any way, and that just made her sad because they missed out on a completely different level of relationship with people. She knew that most of the time the other people didn't care. Most of the time, they didn't want anything other than what they had. That's because they didn't have any experience in assisting others; they didn't know what they were missing out on. More so, they didn't know what it would take to give back to others.

As sad as that sounded, Clary also knew that a lot of people didn't care. They were only thinking about themselves at the time, and that was it. She sat here, waiting as her energy was pulled and buffeted, and she just kept it at bay. She was waiting for him to end the flow himself, so as not to interfere while he wielded it, until he didn't need it anymore.

She got bits and pieces, glimpses of what was going on, but she put up a baffle to mute some of the urgency. He needed to not be panicked by things she didn't understand, and it was bound to distract him, if he could feel her overbearing presence as well. She needed to protect him but also had to trust that these guys could take care of their business. It was apparent; they did it well enough.

The fact that they had been attacked and taken out once before, shouldn't have been criticism at all. They worked well together, but, of course, it was much harder to keep her mind away from the thought of it happening again.

She knew they were up on the roof, looking for the snipers. And this odd tension in the room around her couldn't be undone. These others in the room had helped, and all that mattered at the moment was letting the team handle it. She saw Tasha and Sophia were hard at work on the computer monitors, doing everything they could to help the men outside.

Clary didn't want to get in their way, so she stayed with Cara, Lorelei, and Mariana, who was doing what she did best—stress-baking to take her mind off everything else.

Of course they would all benefit from that. Clary loved the fact that somebody enjoyed cooking. It was great because there was nothing quite like food to bolster moods.

Mariana had Little Calum with her as well.

Clary thought better of joining the other women in the kitchen cooking and stayed clear. Computers were not really her thing either, so she just stayed at the counter, watching Little Calum and Mariana.

Clary knew perfectly well who she would be protecting, if and when the time came. As far as she was concerned, adults made their own decisions. Clary would help as far as she could to save everyone, but it was the little one who would need the most help. He would also be the easiest to work with.

She loved that. It didn't take long for Mariana to notice Clary's pensive gaze.

"Problems?" she asked quietly, walking over with a cookie for Clary.

Clary looked at the cookies and laughed lightly. "I was just thinking about how nice it is that somebody here cooks as their way of handling stress."

Mariana grinned. "Right, it's not necessarily a good thing either, when all I do is cook all the damn time," she muttered, shaking her head, "but, hey, for me, it works, so I'm good with it."

"Works for all of us, and I, for one, am most grateful."

She chuckled. "I don't know about grateful, but it does seem to be something that puts a smile on everybody's face."

"And that's a—wow!" Clary stopped midsentence and looked at Mariana, shocked.

"What? What's going on?" Mariana asked, alarmed.

Clary shook her head, holding up the cookie in her hand. "Oh, nothing's wrong, but wow. These things are magic."

"I didn't know they could work wonders like that. Suddenly you are smiling."

"These are amazing." Clary smiled even while she ate.

"Are you sure?"

"Yes. It's true. It's interesting that something so small can have that effect on people."

"I think any well-prepared food can do that." Mariana looked over at Little Calum, who was curled up in a chair and nodding off. He had a book in his hands, but his eyelids kept closing and then would jolt open. He was trying so hard to stay awake and to read some more.

"He really fights naptime, doesn't he?" Clary murmured.

"Absolutely. So much is going on all the time, and he just wants to be a part of it," Mariana noted.

"That's understandable. I think we all want to be a part of it, but maybe just not like this. He is particularly determined." She gave a wave of her hand.

Mariana nodded in understanding. "You brought a very interesting skill set to the place."

She grinned. "Well, my sister did before me, if we're to be honest."

"Yes, absolutely," Mariana agreed, "and yours seems just a little bit more advanced, from what I can understand."

"No, not at all. Just a little different." She had always wanted to keep it a secret, but it was already out. "That's the thing. Even though we're sisters, it's still something similar and yet different."

"Right," Mariana murmured. "It's fascinating though."

"What about you?" Clary stared at her.

"I knew immediately when Calum was hurt with the team," she shared. "And I had absolutely no compunction about getting up and flying over here because I knew it was serious. But, as far as the depth of that energy connection? I don't think it's more than that."

"Or you just haven't worked on it yet."

"Possibly that too," Mariana agreed. "It seems growing, and I thought it was just because now we're together, whereas before it was a much more uncertain relationship."

"Yet probably in your head, you weren't sure that it was uncertain as much as you just needed a chance to sort things out."

"That is quite true," Mariana said, "but, because we

needed to sort things out, it always gave us both the impression that we weren't together."

Clary nodded in agreement. "Those kinds of things are a struggle too. You think you've got it. You hope you've got it, but then you find out you haven't got anything."

Mariana chuckled. "Exactly. And, for all our attempts to work things out before, it just never happened because we were on different planes—but that's not how it is now."

"Good," Clary declared. "Even thinking that you two had problems is sad. I'm glad you're together. Little Calum here will benefit tremendously from having his dad around."

"Oh, he absolutely will." Mariana smiled. "He has already, and I think his dad will too."

"No doubt."

With that, Mariana leaned forward and whispered, "How much danger are we in?"

"A lot," Clary confirmed cheerfully, "but I have faith."

Immediately Mariana appeared a bit lost. "It's just an interesting space and time right now."

"And not terribly comforting, is it?" Clary murmured.

"It really isn't. I have one focus right now, and that's to keep my son safe," Mariana stated. "At the same time, I don't want my focus diverted, nor Calum's. I would hate to distract his father and put him at risk."

"I don't think that'll happen. If anything, I think it probably makes him even more focused because he's never had anything quite so precious to lose before."

"That's a good way for me to look at it," Mariana noted. "I'm really looking forward to our life together, when this is all over."

"What do you see that life being?" Clary asked curiously.

Mariana looked at her, surprised. "You know what? I

guess I hadn't projected what that would be like. I guess I was seeing something without all this stress and pain, just having more time to be together."

"I think our time will come," she noted consolingly.

"I'm just not sure what that new lifestyle will look like. Honestly I'd be totally okay to have a big complex like this," she said. "I mean, I'm not sure I want to sign up to do the cooking for everybody all the time"—she laughed—"but I'm certainly okay to do it part-time, and, if we had help, … that would be great."

"So, you see the team staying together?" Clary asked curiously.

At that, Mariana looked around, nodding. "I don't know how it would happen or what it would look like from a business perspective or anything, but I can't see a scenario that has these guys separating. They are very close, like brothers. … You have your sister, so you already know how that feels. I just can't envision these guys going their separate ways any more than I could see you and Cara separating." Mariana gave Clary a questioning gaze. "Wouldn't you want to stay close to your sister?"

"Oh God, absolutely," Clary stated, with a bright smile. "If we can make that happen, it would be a huge blessing. I'm just not sure what that'll look like."

"And I don't think we're meant to know just yet," Mariana suggested. "Some things we have to take on faith." And, with that, she got up and quickly walked over to catch Little Calum before he fell out of his chair. She gently scooped him up into her arms, then looked over at Clary. "I think it's time for a nap." And she quickly carried him down the hallway.

Clary watched which room they went into, took note of

it, and then sat back and relaxed. At least she knew where they were, if that became an issue. She didn't want it to be, but some things were just ingrained. As she sat here waiting, Lorelei came in, looked at her in surprise.

"Are you sitting all alone out here?" she asked.

"Yeah, Mariana just went to put her son down for a nap," she explained.

"Ah, that makes sense, and it's probably for the best." Lorelei hesitated but walked toward Clary. "So, how are you doing?"

"I'm doing okay," she murmured. "It's a lot of people to get to know all at once. Definitely more than I'm used to, but I'm working on it."

Lorelei smiled. "But you know we can't really expect anything else from any of us at this point," she murmured. "We've all been through a lot, you included."

"There are a lot of great things about being a part of this group, and I can see that there would also be some frustrations," Clary noted. "It'll just take a little bit of time and some adjustment."

"How are you and Brody getting along?"

Clary realized that was one of several burning questions they all must have. *Would she and Brody hook up? Would she be that missing partner and become part of the group? Would they split as soon as he was healed?* "I think we're doing okay," she replied quietly. "Obviously this is not something that either of us expected or pursued, and, in some ways, I think he feels like it was put on him, without his getting a choice in the matter."

"Oh, gosh," Lorelei said. "I hadn't thought about that, but you're right. I mean, all these decisions were made in a time of need. That's not exactly something Brody really cares about now though, is it?"

Clary chuckled. "I don't think so, no. It's all good for now. We're getting there, and it will only get better as he heals and doesn't feel like he's so dependent, you know?"

"Yes, that makes sense," Lorelei agreed. "Yet it can't be easy. These men aren't used to relying on anyone else for anything."

"No, that's true. So how are things with you?"

"We're good." She smiled. "Better than good. Honestly, if I'd had the slightest inkling things could be this good, I would have tried to make it happen earlier."

"I wonder if that works?" Clary asked.

"I don't know," Lorelei replied. "Probably not. We all still have some things to work out. We're all still figuring out our new relationships in a time of crisis, except for Mariana—and maybe Damon and Tasha to a degree. They worked together, but they weren't *together*, together by any means. Just the opposite, in fact."

"Well, even still, they were developing a lot of energy bonds while they weren't *together*, together," Clary noted, chuckling. "Even I can see that."

Lorelei frowned. "See? That's the thing. There is so much to learn here. So many things to develop and to grow, like the connections some are talking about. It makes me worried that some are so far advanced, possibly putting pressure on the others, which is bound to be hard," she added.

"Everyone will find their own way, and I would tell anyone not to stress over it," Clary offered, sensing the insecurity Lorelei felt. "As the energy grows, growing with it will be easier and faster for everybody else as well."

"Meaning that I could also grow and do more?" she

asked hopefully.

"Absolutely," Clary declared. "That's how energy works. And, when you get a collective like us together, it will grow even faster. Everyone won't be the same, just like the abilities of the men are each a bit different."

"Well, it would be hard to argue with that," Lorelei murmured. "I really would like to do more and to learn more."

"So just allow yourself the freedom to do so," Clary suggested. "I know that sounds simplistic, and, in many ways it is, but it's also quite true. Many people hold off on what they can do because they don't think they can or should or whatever other craziness is in their mind. Holding yourself back is not an option because, if you stress over it, then you don't grow."

"Right, so it's about giving yourself permission?" Lorelei asked.

"Absolutely," Clary murmured. "Don't hold back. Give yourself whatever permission you need to get there. Then just open yourself up to the possibilities."

"Good thought," Lorelei said. "I'm really glad I asked."

"I suspect that, *if* we all stay and work together"—Clary put emphasis on *if*—"there will potentially be a lot of things we could learn from each other."

"Can you teach me some of that?"

"I've never tried," Clary admitted honestly, "but I'd be the first one to say that anything is possible, especially if the heart is there."

Lorelei chuckled. "You know what? I think you're right. And there's a ton of heart in this group. I'd really hate to see it come to pass in any another form. There is a tremendous amount of love to be given."

"But also a tremendous amount of love to be received," Clary added. "We just have to work a little harder on it."

"I'd like that too." Lorelei got up to pour herself a cup of coffee. She looked over at Clary and smiled. "Do you want some?"

"No thanks, I'm good for now," she murmured.

Lorelei hesitated, then asked, "Have you had anything to do with what's going on out there?"

"No," she replied calmly, "but I'm really struggling to stay out of it."

"I get that," Lorelei agreed. "I really do because that's why I'm sitting here too. It's so hard to keep my head straight, and my thoughts are all over the place."

"Absolutely, it's almost impossible," Clary noted.

"You're not getting anything?"

"Gage's fine. That's all I can tell you."

"Well, that's good." Lorelei sighed. "As long as he's fine, then nothing else is blowing up. I'll head back to my work." Then she turned and disappeared from the doorway. Clary wanted to know what that work was, but then remembered something about Lorelei still working with the US government, like with the CIA or something.

As soon as she was alone, Clary closed her eyes and sent out a probe toward Brody. It was one thing to say that all was fine; it was another to loosen up the guard. She needed to know for sure that he was okay because she knew that he was in a stressful scenario that could go either way at a moment's notice.

Once she reconnected with his energy, she saw it flowing steadily. He didn't appear to be under any undue stress. As their connection was made and their energy interacted, she saw something happening, something that had his energy flaring.

She just kept a calm eye on it.

As long as he didn't utilize too much energy, he would be fine, but, as soon as he got into trouble, there would be no end to it. She could feel her own muscles tensing, as he exerted himself more.

She could only do so much from a distance like this, however, so she just sat here tense and aware that whatever was happening out there was not getting serious. She didn't know how to stop it or what she was supposed to do about it anyway, except sit here and wait. There was a hope that the team would solve any problems on their own.

It wasn't something she particularly wanted to be involved in, partly because she knew she wouldn't come up with the same kind of solutions that they would, and any intervention by her during one of their ops would put them in more danger. She wanted to be part of a solution, not causing more problems in the midst of heavy fire.

While she struggled with the idea of doing nothing, she finally eased back ever-so-slightly, then got what almost seemed like *Thanks.*

Something that said she was valuable and recognizable, from Brody. She smiled at that and sent him a wave of smiling energy. Almost at the same time, she felt his energy hit a hard wall or like something had hit him, and then his energy level dropped and kept dropping.

She poured her energy toward him and bolted to her feet, turning to look around the area, wondering just what was going on. It was way too intense for some kind of feedback and too early to assess what was going on.

All she got was nothing, no trouble in sight hitting the fan. She didn't have any visual on this. She noted that

Brody's energy was depleting at top speed, as if he were under extreme pressure or anxiety.

Any kind of attack would send him running for cover. It would send anybody running for cover. Who was she kidding? The last thing she wanted to do was go up there and deal with that kind of crap herself.

She closed her eyes and sent calming and focused energy his way. She wasn't sure it would do any good, but she would take what little bit of progress she could get.

Almost immediately she sensed some of Brody's energy calming down. Yet she wasn't sure if it was his energy or the effect of hers. She thought it was probably from the calming effect.

The learning curve was steep with Brody. He had abilities that she hadn't even considered when mixed up in a personal relationship. He could be doing some of this himself.

In fact, she might be counteracting what she was hoping to accomplish, what Brody was hoping to accomplish. Frowning, she sensed still more shit happening, as his heart rate picked up and his pulse took off. Then she felt some erratic energy pattern throwing her off-balance.

She didn't know what the hell was happening, and she needed more information. Just as she started to panic, the door opened, and Sophia came racing in.

"How is he?" she cried out. "How are any of them?"

"Wade's fine," Clary stated.

"Tasha's monitoring it on the satellite," Sophia said.

"What's going on? What's happening?" Clary bolted up to her feet and raced over to Sophia.

"By the looks of it, they're under attack."

"In that case," Clary stated, "I'm heading over to be with

Mariana and Calum."

Sophia looked at her in shock. "Do you think somebody is inside?"

"I don't know," she admitted, "but protecting them, as I support Brody, is my best role. You go back and see if you can hold steady with whatever is coming."

"Shit." Sophia stopped in the doorway. "Do you have a weapon?"

"No, of course not." Then seeing the look of dismay on Sophia's face, Clary continued. "Sophia"—she sent a wave of calm over to her—"I don't need one."

Sophia's eyebrows shot up. "Okay, we'll *so* have to talk about this later."

"We definitely can. I promise. But, right now, we're under attack, and we've got jobs to do," Clary murmured.

"Let's see if we can put a stop to this. I've already had about enough of this bullshit," Sophia said.

"Hey, I'm all for that," Clary agreed softly.

"I don't mind doing various missions," Sophia stated, "but this kind of stuff gets old real quick."

"It gets old because we're desperately trying to get to an end point we haven't been able to see yet," Clary replied.

"Got it," Sophia muttered, and, with that, she was gone.

Clary took a deep breath and walked herself down to the bedroom door, where Mariana and Calum were resting. She wanted to open it and see if they were okay, but she could already sense the two bodies inside.

Only two. And that was the part she needed to know.

She sat down in the hallway on the floor, closed her eyes, and worked hard with her energy to camouflage anybody on the inside.

Their attackers would be coming in through the other

entrance, and it would take them past her to the offices on the other end. She was hoping she could neutralize whoever was coming before the bad guys got that far.

She needed to; somebody needed to stop them. Just way too much was going on here for the group to keep going in a frenzied fear.

She could do this.

Thinking over and over in her head, her heartbeat slowed. She'd never utilized energy as a weapon but only as a healing tool. Yet, as soon as she realized how much danger they were in, she had no problem turning that healing tool into something that could kill.

She just hoped she didn't have to use it in that way.

She knew such an event would be a stain on her soul that she would have a hard time dealing with. But to protect others, there was absolutely no doubt. She had gone to the other side and had crossed over, with her foot straddling the abyss. If she were to do it protecting them, she would.

She couldn't stand the thought of living without them. So it wasn't all that far off to contemplate this. The thought that she could drop somebody over on the other side wasn't as shocking as it seemed. She sent out a probe for her sister and immediately found the answering probe waiting for her.

I'm in the computer room, she heard Cara say. *You protect those two, and I'll protect the ones here. Join our energies as a shield.*

With that, connected as always, they both waited.

BRODY HID BEHIND the wall and poked his head out once to check where the sniper was.

The outline of a figure disappeared behind a wall again. The snipers could keep them pinned down for hours at this rate. Just then the sniper fired again, the shot hitting the cement in front of his head. It had to come from the opposite direction, so he ducked, pulling back even farther out of harm's way and hopefully out of both snipers' line of sight.

Terk called out, "You okay?"

"Yep. Second sniper at nine o'clock."

"Yeah, I see him." Terk swore. "How many more do they have?"

"You'd think they would have run out of assholes by now."

Just then, one of the snipers yelled, "Give it up, Terk. We've waited a long time for this."

Everyone froze. Talk about making it personal.

Terk called back, "Too bad I don't even know who you are. Doesn't that take all the fun out of it?"

It was smart of Terk to engage him.

"Well, you know what? … Maybe some of it." He laughed. "Just not all of it though. We got your girlfriend too."

Terk froze. "Are you sure about that? Seems odd since I don't have one," he called back in a calm, steady voice.

Brody always appreciated that about his boss. Nothing seemed to ever set him off. Although Brody imagined that finding out about Celia for the first time would have thrown Terk off his game. At least as much as anything would.

"Well, well, she's in Texas. Just thought you should know," the sniper said, "but we also know where she is. We let her go, but she is close enough. We wanted to make sure that we knew where she ended up. And you can bet that we've got a plan in action for her too."

Brody swore in his head. He knew that Levi and Ice's compound would be ready for any attack, particularly if they were still looking after Celia. But Brody also knew this was deliberately geared to pull Terk's attention off the ball here and in a whole different direction.

"That's nice," Terk called back in a bored voice. "Haven't you guys run out of assholes to do your dirty work yet? Killed any of them recently?"

"Nope. But you know something? … There's always enough stupid idiots out there in the world," he snapped, and then went on to add, "Just like you guys."

"Yeah, well, we also know you're tied to the Iran operation," Brody yelled.

At that came a shocked surprise before the sniper replied again. His tone was furious, ugly, and almost gargling. "You think you know something, do you?" he asked. "You don't know jack shit. You took out my brother in that little fiasco of yours. And, for that, I'll make sure I take out your brother, Terk. An eye for an eye, bitch."

"Apparently you want to take out everybody," Terk corrected, "every team member, every relationship, everything."

"Yep. You do it to me," he replied, "and I'll do it twenty times worse to you."

Just then, several more shots were fired, and Brody could only hope that none of them found their mark. When Terk called back again, Brody realized it had just been random fire from a pissed-off gunman.

Those were always the worst—and the most dangerous too.

"Now what? What do you want?" Terk asked.

"I want you dead," the gunman yelled. "How could you

possibly think it was anything other than that?"

"No can do," Terk noted. "You have gone through a lot of hoops to get here. Made a lot of trouble trying to take us out, but so far it hasn't worked."

"That's because I've been hiring idiots," he grumbled in a disgusted tone. "Who knew they could all be so bad?"

"I don't know about that. I think your drone operator was pretty decent, but then he had to be taken out. Why was that? You can't manage to keep one person safe? And then you had the punks and the IT people who had second thoughts about what they were doing. You should have seen their faces when they finally realized what they could get arrested for." Terk laughed.

"You know that it just makes our paychecks so much bigger when you don't have to split them."

"Ah, paychecks," Terk noted. They were pinned down at the moment, but getting the information seemed a good bargain for their trouble. "So this is more than just a vendetta on your part. You're getting paid to do this."

"Hey, two birds with one stone," he said. "Why wouldn't I?"

"I suppose," Terk shouted back. "You want to tell me who it is who wants us all dead so bad?"

"Nope, I think not," he replied. "Something in the contract about not telling too much. Not that I give a shit. I just think it's better for you to keep worrying about it."

"Hardly worrying, when it's all your own men lying dead all over," Terk noted. "MI6 is quite pissed at you."

"I'm sure they're quite pissed at you too." He laughed again. "It's only because you're here that they are having to deal with all the bodies."

"Maybe." Terk's voice was calm, sounding almost disinterested.

Brody searched the horizon, looking for any sign of the other sniper. This time he was armed and not with a pistol. He raised his rifle and searched ever-so-slowly through the scope. There wouldn't be much chance to react, and, when he got the opportunity for a shot, he would take it. He was the only one on this side of the building who could.

He heard Terk call out, "Besides, what's the fun in that? Surely a man deserves to know who's trying to kill him."

"What? You don't know me?" he asked.

"Yeah, of course I do," Terk replied. "You're Yousef."

Again came more silence and then a bitter laugh. "Well, at least you know my name." He didn't seem to worry about any repercussions.

"Your brother was creating a weapon to take out a large portion of the US and had created a group of men like us, but with mass annihilation on their mind. Plus had also created a machine, modeled after your brother's special team. So that men like that—like you—couldn't have such unholy power," Terk explained. "What were you expecting me to do? Should I have slapped his hand instead? What were you expecting the government to do, for that matter?"

"He hadn't gotten far enough to even be called danger-ous," Yousef yelled, "so it's hardly likely you guys were even aware of what he was doing."

"We were aware," Terk admitted, "but it sounds like maybe you weren't aware of how far down that pathway your brother was."

"Zaid was not a terrorist!" Yousef cried out in fury. "He was a genius and gifted."

"Maybe, if that's the word you want to use," Terk replied, "but you know perfectly well that his invention was functioning at a preliminary level because you used it against us."

"Of course I did," Yousef yelled. "You deserved it. You took out an innocent man. A man with a family. You took him from his wife, and you orphaned two boys," he cried out. "Why should you decide they would be left without a husband and a father? Who are you to make that choice? He was a good man."

"A good man in the wrong field," Terk noted. "Just like all of you."

He laughed hysterically. "Absolutely. Do you like your little present?"

"If you mean the woman," Terk replied, "not particularly. And it's not certain that the child is mine. It could be anybody's for that matter."

"Nope, it's yours," Yousef declared. "But that of course … that was all something I owed my brother."

"What are you talking about?" Terk said.

And for the first time, Yousef said something that threw Terk off-balance, and it showed in his tone. There was something about this conversation that was getting to Terk, and that was not good. Brody immediately sent out a message, warning Terk to stay calm.

"That sperm," Yousef stated, "you're probably thinking that your brother, … that maybe he got a little careless and had an affair, but that's not what happened. It's your sperm, your child." Yousef's tone was menacing.

"How can you be sure?" Terk asked.

"Maybe I'm not. So let's just talk hypothetically."

"Sure. What do you have in mind?"

"Suppose a guy donates his sperm or maybe a sample is obtained."

"Obtained how?"

"That's not part of the story, is it?" He continued. "My guess is that the sperm samples were on ice for future use."

"But what if the sperm came from nobody? What if no one gave a shit about the sperm donor?" Terk asked.

"What if the guy was the leader of a black ops group?"

"So, you're just fishing. Anybody's sperm could have been used. Drop the hypotheticals. You sure didn't need mine."

"Nope. That's true. We could have just said it was yours, but you know it's much nicer this way," Yousef said, "because it is yours, and she has no idea what happened to her. She wasn't part of your world at all, which is even more fun."

"How so?" Terk asked.

"Because she's a complete innocent. Although she was someone my brother picked, so maybe she wasn't completely innocent. And that's even better too if she was."

"What do you mean?"

"Something about needing to test her. He'd picked her up and was doing tests on her. That's when he realized that he had something he could use to pressure you long enough for them to finish this weapon of theirs."

Yousef was sharing more than they could handle from here, but it was something.

"How is it that Zaid knew about the weapon?" Terk asked, calm again. "You said it yourself. He wasn't a terrorist."

"Because he wasn't. He was working on a harmless project and rushed to complete it because the word was out that something was coming. It was you who made this nightmare. He figured you were after him too. When you took out the entire team, he was proven right. I should tell you that he didn't live very long, and he wasn't in great shape, but he lived long enough to set his revenge plan in motion." Yousef's voice was cracking. "And then Zaid died. And I took over to make sure my brother was avenged."

At that, Brody winced because that meant that the poor woman, Celia, had been picked up, held against her will for a long time, and then, as a final trick, they had inseminated her.

She had no idea what the hell had prompted this attack on her.

She was a victim in all this, proving again that these people didn't care about hurting more people. His heart went out to the poor woman who was unaware, innocent, and dragged into a mess not of her making. Even now, a full-on attack was coming her way that she had nothing to do with.

Brody hoped Terk could keep his cool long enough to get as much information as they could. He wasn't doing bad so far, but they needed so much more.

"So, this is all about the attack the government set up on your brother's group in Iran?" Terk asked. "So why is it that you're not pissed at the American government for it?"

"Well, you can't really fight governments, even if you want to," Yousef explained, "and at the end of the day, you don't have a whole lot of power. We could pull another terrorist attack and bring down some big monument. We could kill a few thousand more Americans," Yousef replied, "but the way you guys populate, it wouldn't make a damn bit of difference. You'd be back up and running in no time. Old tricks, new faces," he said, "but we have something much, much better happening right now."

"You mean this?" Terk asked once again, with that bored tone, as if this Yousef guy was wasting his time. "There are always better snipers in the world. You are not it, man. You are nothing. Nada, zilch, dude. Not a big deal."

"Sure," Yousef agreed. "Snipers were my brother's specialty and so much more, Terk. And the best part is, we're getting paid for it."

"If you live to get paid. Remember that. So you still haven't told me why, or who is paying you for it."

"Nope," he said, "but I did leave you hints today, if you can survive me first. Not that you'll necessarily figure it out. By the way, I'm planning on you not surviving." More gunfire rang out, peppering everyone on the roof with a spray of bullets.

But again it looked like it was just for show. It was temporary gunfire, and Terk's team was struggling against an adversary intent on mocking them.

Brody couldn't see the second gunman, and there was no guarantee that he was even still around. Brody wanted to go to the other rooftop, but getting into the stairwell and getting out of here wasn't really an option at this point either. Something else in a long list of things pissing him off.

Just enough was going on here that he wanted to help Terk get as much information as he could.

"Yeah, it's the person who's paying you that's of interest to me," Terk noted, "and considering you're not expecting any of us to survive, why bother with a hint? Why not just tell us?"

"Nope," Yousef said. "That's all you get."

"Fine, do your worst."

There was a startled moment of silence from the talkative sniper, then Yousef spat, "You think this is just fun and games? Do you think that I did all this for nothing, just to sit here and talk to you?"

Brody shook his head. Yousef was batshit crazy but still building his anger, like just before a raging storm.

"Do you think I have no second plan or no end game?"

"I'm sure you think you do," Terk said.

"Do you really think that the people you're protecting inside that building are safe?" And Yousef started to laugh.

At that, Brody's blood ran cold and then hot. He was thrust into agony, and he felt everything inside him freeze. After all they'd been through, he knew deep down and had expected that their attackers would attempt to get inside. But, with three of the team up on the roof, being held down by snipers, plus Rick and Cal standing guard at the ground-floor doors, Brody wondered how many men it would take to defend those inside the building. And at what point in time would it happen?

He raised his weapon against the far wall and waited, feeling so much better that at least he was armed now. He heard the conversation still going on around him, with Terk's patient attempts to try and get more information and the other guy's unwillingness to part with it. All starting to grate on Brody's nerves.

"You know what I always wondered?" Yousef asked. "I always wondered what you found good about working for the government. You should know that they'll betray you in a heartbeat for their own agenda."

"Is that what yours did?" Terk asked quietly.

Brody knew that this was the burning question they'd all been wanting to know. Had the very government they had served done this to Terk's team?

Yousef laughed. "I just think it's the nature of the beast," he stated in almost a mocking tone of voice. "The minute you find anybody who knows too much, they can't be left alive."

"Well, that is definitely your motto," Terk noted. "How many of your own guys have you taken out already?"

"As many as I can," he declared. "Man, I'm serious. I don't like to share paychecks."

"Got it," Terk said, almost laughing. "Good to know. Remind me not to do business with you."

"Oh, hell no," he snarled. "Not after you took out my brother."

"So we're to completely forget the fact that he was trying to take all of us out first? Right?"

"Obviously," Yousef stated. "My brother was a special man. And you're just an asshole for taking out that team."

"I didn't think anybody survived that op, to tell you the truth."

"Well, they didn't, at least not for long. Just long enough for Zaid to set plans into motion to make sure you paid for it," Yousef repeated. "When he couldn't even do that job himself, I stepped up to make sure revenge was meted out. I promised him that I would. You should know that I don't take my promises lightly."

Brody could imagine. Some family members were incredibly loyal, and they would risk life and limb to follow through on something that somebody else had started.

"Too bad he was on the wrong side of this," Terk replied. "We aren't looking for weapons to hurt the world."

"Sure, but then when you find them, and you don't like them, you take them out."

"We aren't you, Yousef."

"You're just as bad as anybody else. And all your holier

than thou BS? None of us needs that," Yousef yelled. "Nobody needs it. And the sooner you guys understand it, the better."

"I understand it somewhat," Terk noted. "But, when you're done with us, then what will you do? Do you expect to be at peace?"

"I'll be at peace," Yousef stated instantly, his voice calm and almost centered, as if he was looking forward to that. "Believe me. There will be an end to all this."

"I hope so, for your sake," Terk replied calmly. "The last thing we want to do is to take out anybody else. I am not particularly keen on wiping out an entire family."

"Zaid took his wife and his sons with him already," Yousef stated menacingly. "He felt it was better to take them along, than to leave them here to face whatever nightmare you would rain down on them."

That truth was too much. Brody's heart slammed against his chest, and he knew the rest of them would be shocked as well.

"When you say, Zaid *took them*, what do you mean?" Terk asked.

"He took them to Allah with him. He didn't want to leave them alone. He knew they would suffer here without him."

"He killed his own family?" Terk asked.

Brody heard the damage to Terk's spirit in his voice.

"We don't look at it the same way," Yousef explained, in defense of his brother's actions.

"What about you? Why didn't he take you with him too?"

At that, the other man laughed. "Because I had to finish his work."

"When you finish his work, is it over then?" Terk asked. "Or do you feel like you have to continue in your brother's footsteps too."

"I don't have the same abilities as he did, unfortunately. So that's not an option for me."

For that, Brody was grateful. There were only so many of these guys out there that they wanted to deal with. They had been working through them one at a time, and he had thought they were all gone, but obviously they had one left, one last man left behind.

The last man standing.

They were wrong that the op took out everybody. No one could have predicted this, and it was shocking to even imagine that anybody could survive that op in Iran. They had barely survived it themselves, but that wasn't something that was very well publicized. And it backfired on them in a big way.

The government backlash had been brutal. Not that the government had been worried about Terk's team's survival but only about their team's success.

It had been a sobering realization.

What Yousef had said about working for the government was definitely something that they had all wondered. They were the guardian angels, until something goes wrong. Then they became the fall guys.

Before the Iran operation, they had full government support, and, once they failed in some way to meet expectations, it really didn't matter that they had worked hard for them all this time.

Too damn hard. Now it was all down the drain.

No one could control this.

"Yousef, I'm sorry it fell to you," Terk noted. "It must

be hard being left behind, all alone like this. It must be hard, not being good enough for Zaid to take you with him."

"It wasn't like that," he yelled, his voice rough and angry. "You're just trying to turn them against me."

"Not at all," Terk said. "Obviously the loss of your family has affected you. That Zaid took his own family with him is a little on the unbelievable side from my point of view."

"She wanted to go," Yousef stated casually. "She didn't want to be left behind. And the children couldn't be left alone without their parents."

"Is it because she knew there would be a government investigation and they would end up in jail?"

"It's possible," Yousef admitted. "My brother always operated just ever-so-slightly under the radar. He did what was allowed. He'd had government support for a time, and, when that was pulled, he continued his noble cause on his own."

"I hope it was worth it," Terk said.

"It was worth it," Yousef cried out passionately. "My brother was a genius."

"Sure, but, at the end of the day, nobody survived, so how much of a genius was he?" Terk asked, lowering his voice. "You can kill everyone in your world, but, when you take out your own wife and your own children, it's the end of the line."

"But it was the end of the line that he wanted," Yousef declared, his voice getting ever-so-slightly faint. Then in a much stronger voice, as if having stopped himself from going down that mental pathway, he added, "Besides, it won't matter, as long as I have justified his work and have taken revenge on those who killed them, my work is done too."

"Will you then go join him?"

"No," Yousef replied. "No need for me to do that."

Terk didn't respond for a long moment. Brody had to wonder if it was a case of trying to figure out the psychological aspect or because he was trying to figure out the end game here. When he spoke again, Terk asked, "So, if you kill us now, what about the woman in Texas?"

"Oh, she's marked for death," he said.

"How so? Why would that be an issue?" he asked, trying again for that curious tone of voice.

"Because my brother thought that she should live, so she could be taken out later. He asked me to let her live and then to kill her and your child, one by one." Yousef laughed again. "I was setting things up for down the road. Zaid had a great sense of humor. He knew that there was a chance she could survive this, and he didn't want that to happen. Not for long."

"Of course not," Terk noted, "but that's very long-term thinking."

"Well, that was my brother," Yousef noted. "Long-term thinking is what he did best. He had your number a long time ago. The fact that you didn't even know about him and about what he could do just made him smile all the more."

"Maybe," Terk agreed, "but you haven't really said what your brother was doing either."

"He was creating a weapon that would nullify what you guys could do and, at the same time, could take you guys out. Haven't you figured that out yet?"

"Well, it was a worthy effort when used against us," Terk admitted, "or at least a good try. But, like a lot of your brother's inventions, his plan is still half-realized. We are all alive, and those inventions only do half the work."

At that, Yousef gave a shout of anger. "No! That's not

true. If there was any failing, it was in me applying the weapon."

"Are you sure about that?" Terk asked.

"Zaid did the right thing." A fury washed over Yousef's energy. "You will not be allowed to besmirch my brother's memory."

And that was an interesting take too because this Yousef guy was fully prepared to take the blame for any failure.

"Well, it couldn't have been all that hard to set up," Terk noted. "Weapons need to be simple for anybody to use, so maybe Zaid thought he would be around to use it. Even when he knew he was dying, he must have hoped he would live to that point."

"I made a promise to Zaid that I would take care of it. I would take care of what he couldn't do, and I will," Yousef stated passionately. "You will not be allowed to walk away from this."

"So you plan to kill me now, on this rooftop. Then what difference does it make," Terk asked, "if this woman lives on, that you tell me is carrying my child?"

"Because Zaid wanted to make sure that there would be nothing left. There will be no one left to remember you. So it's not just your woman and child but also your brother."

On that note, another round of gunfire filled the air. Finding the opening, Brody lunged for the stairs and got his foot inside the arch just in time to dodge the bullet slamming into the wall behind him—spraying him with cement and splinters, yet he got down safely.

He sent Terk a message, telling him that he was crossing to the other building. And then he raced down the stairs, took stock of what was going on and what it would take to cross over and to enter the building from below.

This will be hell.

CHAPTER 13

CLARY DIDN'T KNOW what just happened, but something did.

Brody was on the run, causing his energy to flare. She didn't know if he was in trouble or not, and that was something she struggled to sort out. She didn't want to do anything to knock them down, but, at the same time, she also couldn't take a chance of Brody going down because he was taking too many chances.

But she couldn't see whether they were under attack or if this was something completely different. Being blind was hurting her in a big way. She sent a message to her sister asking about it.

No idea.

Her sister's mental note was clear. They didn't have any answers. And just when Clary thought to pull back and to take another look at what Brody was doing, she heard a sound that made her blood run cold. *Someone is inside.*

She immediately stepped in Mariana's bedroom, shut the door, and locked it.

She heard footsteps outside the door. Not just footsteps but heavy footsteps. She gave a passing glance to the thought that maybe it was the team coming back in but ditched that thought almost immediately. No time to be optimistic. Something was menacing about those footfalls; the frenzy was real. And a feeling welled up that she knew all too well by now.

She knew that somebody had found a way inside the building, while everybody else was busy on the roof. Within the chaos, somebody had managed to find a weak spot, and they were in.

Now more than ever, Clary needed every ounce of her energy to help deal with what was about to come. She sent out an immediate warning to her sister and anybody else in the vicinity, including Terk, hoping that, at least for the moment, Brody could look after himself.

Need the energy, the camouflage, to get across that street.

Brody was there, and she knew it, and, if she pulled her energy too early, he wouldn't make it. She sent him one vast dump of energy, warned him what they were up against inside the warehouse, and then shut down.

She pulled on the reserve of energy around her and then brought in all her feelers in preparation for whatever might come through that door. She sat and waited in anticipation.

She felt a heartbeat, strong and close. She wasn't sure whose it was. The feelers were doing something different for her, and she wasn't sure of her own exploits yet. It was the most bizarre sensation she'd felt in a very long time.

She sent out a call to her sister, asking if she could feel it. But it came back negative. It wasn't Brody, and she knew that, but beyond that she didn't think it was any friendlies.

Both Mariana and Little Calum had no idea what was coming. Clary closed her eyes, pulling on as much of the energy as she safely could, and put up the type of camouflage that Brody used. She knew instantly that it worked when the light shimmered and flashed for her.

She needed to keep them separate and away from the

intruders. She didn't know how many men had entered the building, but even one was too much. She immediately sent a probe outside the bedroom door, looking to see who was there.

She needed answers.

Who is out there? How many? What are they after?

She could only hope that she would find answers and soon enough to do some good. Because to have it go south right now would have dangerous consequences for everyone. She had no standard weapon; she had nothing except herself. That had been enough, up until now.

She didn't want to doubt herself now, but not knowing what was coming was enough to set her teeth on edge. Inside the room, the two slumbered gently. When she heard the footsteps stop outside their door, she went rigid, knowing her worst fears were at the door. Almost immediately the handle rattled, when someone tried to open the door.

She'd locked it behind her. She put up as much of a screen as she could, hoping to protect anybody from seeing what was inside. As she did, she caught a glimpse of some recognizable energy. She was wondering if it was possible to take that energy to protect herself and the others in this room with her.

The moment she came in contact with the energy, she realized that the protective energy was a mix of her sister's and maybe Terk's.

They'd both sent probes into the room. She smiled at that because, if there was ever that sense of belonging and caring and loving, it was right now in that moment. When she needed all the help she could get, they were there with her.

The intruder outside her door hesitated, maybe wondering how to make his next move. A locked door often meant something precious was inside. She realized her mistake right away. If the door were open, the intruder wouldn't even know they were here, due to her camouflage.

She waited and then decided that maybe instead of just sitting here and waiting, she could do more. She closed her eyes and gently sent out a message. *Nothing is here. Keep walking. Keep walking. Keep walking.*

She wasn't sure if it would have any effect and then realized she didn't want them walking toward the others either. She quickly turned to send out a feeling of loss and wrapped a message inside.

The place is empty. Leave.

The compound is abandoned. Leave.

And, in a continuous hypnotic motion, she just kept sending out the same message over and over again, hoping that anyone outside would pick up that same message and would react as suggested.

She kept sending out the message. There seemed to be just nothing but confusion on the other side, which was better than somebody bursting in and firing at them. Just when she thought she was winning the battle, a hand went back to the door and pulled on it again.

She sucked in a breath, and then, as she waited, she heard another voice behind her call out, "Mommy?"

She knew all her efforts were lost.

BRODY SWORE WHEN he realized that somebody had entered the building.

Everybody was on high alert, but that didn't mean

much. A lot of Terk's people were in there, and, if these assholes had sent one person, that was one thing. Brody trusted the rest of his team to take them out.

But what if they'd sent in a killing squad?

He couldn't hear anything, and he knew that he was on his own at the moment. She'd also shut down her constant energy wave.

She needed it herself.

Whatever it was, this was serious. He felt a loss, a feeling of emptiness without her energy around him. A keen sense of loss that he'd never expected to experience before now heavily weighed him down. It was bizarre, and yet he understood; she was trying to protect the others in the group.

He needed to sweep through the building next door and fast. He pushed ahead to the stairs, moving up as fast as he could to the roof. Only one sniper was up here, with the other one directly on the building 180 degrees in front of him. He also knew Damon had headed up to that one. With any luck, they could take out both snipers at once. And he had to trust that those in the building would be okay on their own.

Clary and Cara will keep them safe.

Brody was prepared to take out his sniper right now. Yet just so much was going on, and their team had so many people to protect. This was the moment. He knew this was the chance to get out of this hole, and the path was clear, yet the chances for success were slim, and he needed to be vigilant. Clary's lack of energy and presence had him doubting, questioning.

At that, another voice slammed into his head and told him to stop overthinking.

Keep it together, Brody. I am not listening to this BS.

He was startled for a moment and then grinned, as he raced up the stairs to the roof door. Terk could work magic on lifting any spirit.

Just checking to make sure you're there, Brody quipped.

I'm here too, she said, sounding like she was right beside Brody, her voice powerfully soothing and, at the same time, he sensed that she was rattled.

Were you under attack?

Yeah. Her voice was curt and sharp. *Not yet but any second now.* He swore at that, and then she added, *You just keep doing what you doing. We'll be fine.*

He wasn't sure how *fine* anybody could be if they were coming under attack. This wasn't her world, and it's not something she should ever have been exposed to. But he'd been the idiot who had insisted on coming home well ahead of time. He's the one who exposed her to danger.

Not something he'd really thought out in the long-term, and, now that she was facing this mess, it made him realize just how much his own rash behavior affected everybody else.

Her voice, dry and yet slightly distracted, emerged like silk on his nerves, soothing him. *Save the moratorium for later. I'll accept your apology when we are all out of this, together.*

Once again, she made him smile because there was just such honesty and a caustic hint to her voice. So pure.

He always knew where he stood with her. She wasn't full of lies and never made any attempt to dissuade him from the path that he was on.

What would be the point? she asked, her voice equally hard.

Good. So glad to hear we understand each other, he murmured.

Clary huffed. *You are hardheaded, and, if we hadn't come when we did, you would have been a mess. You still think that you're separate from me, but you haven't figured out that we're already joined. Joined in a way that I don't even know I can disengage from.* A note of sadness filled her tone.

And what if I don't want you to disengage? Brody asked her.

But you haven't made it clear that you don't want me to. So there's this weird sense of straddling between two different worlds.

And I'm sorry about that. Let's take care of these attacks, and we'll discuss it.

I'm working on it.

What are you doing, Clary?

At the moment, silencing the little one. I just put him back to sleep. He called out for a moment, at a very inopportune time, and we've got shit hitting the fan. The best thing would be if he could sleep through the whole thing.

Yeah, I hear you. I'm on the same page, and I'm working on it.

Our intruder is on the other side of this bedroom door. I don't want to keep the door locked because that will just bring more interest to this room, but neither do I have any intention of letting him get in here.

I would really appreciate it if you had a way to stop them from getting in. I really don't even know what I can do.

None of us does, not until we're put to the test.

Brody realized just how true that was and how honest of her to acknowledge that she didn't know what she could and could not do in this scenario. *I have faith in your abilities. I'm coming out on the adjacent roof, looking for the shooter.*

There are two, she said, her tone urgent, as if she had just found that piece of information.

I know, and three of us are up here, but two of us are targeting the two different shooters. Damon's on the big-mouthed one, and I've gone after the other one on the adjacent building.

God, it's the waiting that kills me.

I know.

Now I need to disconnect so I can focus. And, if you don't need to pull on me, please don't. If you need to, ... well, I'll already know, and it will be in progress.

And, with that, she disappeared from his head. The fact that she could even do that said something about her abilities that he hadn't even considered before. It's like these two women were on the same level as Terk, and they hadn't realized it yet.

Brody hadn't even considered just how important they were to the survival of the team, the whole group, but, if they didn't have Clary right now, Brody couldn't imagine who would be protecting Little Calum and Mariana. Obviously everybody would have been shepherded into one building at the last moment.

Or, if they'd had a little more time, they could have carried everybody out, potentially safe, but at what cost? With Cara and Clary, everyone on the inside was potentially safe. *We have to end this.*

Brody couldn't even imagine what Terk would do regarding this whole scenario because all the people in their expanded group meant so much to Terk. To all of them. Brody also knew what losing his brother would do to Terk. He would deem it his own fault and would be devastated. It was not something he would argue about, but Brody also knew that no way would Terk ever let himself off the hook for Merk's death.

That made it even harder for Terk, so Brody knew that he needed to act decisively. They were one, and they knew right from wrong. The Iran operation had been carried out by the team, per their government's orders. They did that op together, which meant that they created this monster together. It wasn't only Terk's doing, and now they would end it together.

For the team.

The situation was pissing Brody off, and, without neutralizing Yousef, there was no safety for any of them. Brody stepped out on the roof, rifle at the ready, and slipped up to the end of the huge metal stacks from the HVAC system. He heard a conversation still going on outside.

"It doesn't even matter," the gunman stated. "I know you're all trying to figure out how to stop me." Yousef shook his head. "But it won't happen, and, even if it does, it doesn't matter because so many things are in play right now. You won't stop them all."

Then Yousef stepped out of Brody's sight.

"But, hey, go ahead and give it your best shot. The good old try that you seem to think you can do. You always thought you guys were the best of the best," Yousef said, "but you're not even close. We studied you. We took notes on all of it. We made sure that we understood exactly what was happening in Iran, and now we have taken a page out of your playbook, Terk. You guys have been one step behind us this whole way, and we've seen it every damn time. We did something you never expected. We laughed the whole time, as we took out all the different people we hired."

Yousef continued. "Everybody who thought that they

were something, who needed to be part of something big, are all dead," he murmured, "because there is no *something* after this."

"What will you do with the weapon when you're gone?" Terk asked.

"It's already arranged for sale," he murmured. "I just have to survive this, and then I can live the life that my brother always wanted for his family."

"You mean the life *he* wanted, if he hadn't been so intent on trying to kill all of us."

"Only because you killed so many of his team. You destroyed everything he worked for. His family, his work, then you killed him as well. The lab was under contract for the government, and he didn't have any choice, but you guys didn't care, as long as you took them out."

On the roof and still hidden from sight, Brody took stock of the situation. On the roof of the other building, he saw Damon opening the door and stepping out. So far, they were both out in the clear, but Brody knew that wouldn't last. The minute they were seen, it would be an all-out war.

"He's in hand," Brody reported.

"I see mine too," Damon replied.

When they hit go time, they sent Terk a message. When Brody came out of his hiding spot, almost immediately a weapon fired and hit the concrete at his feet.

He didn't even react and rolled ahead, firing at his target. It all happened so fast that, by the time he stopped his own advance, he didn't appear to have a scratch on him. Whether that was his own skill or Clary's intervention, he didn't know, but he was grateful.

Terk immediately asked for an assessment.

"I'm fine." Brody then waited for Damon to check-in,

and, when he did, they realized it was good—so far. "Now what?" Brody muttered to himself, as he turned and looked.

Let's end this.

There are gunmen in the compound.

Mine is still alive and kicking, Damon alerted them.

Using Terk for his eyes, Brody quickly raced along the top of the roof, looking for that opportunity to get close enough to take out the other gunman. Yousef stood up suddenly and started firing, but Brody was already rolling and moving out of the line of fire, and, by the time he came to a stop, he heard the other guy swearing.

"It won't matter, Terk," Yousef cried out. "Too much is in motion, and you'll never get your happily ever after."

Terk asked him, "Don't you want to just give it up and just go?"

"Won't matter if I do or not," Yousef said. "I have to avenge my brother. So, if you can take me out, then take me out."

"You'd still avenge him, even though he was a mad scientist?"

At that, he laughed. "Yes."

"You know that's not the way to live, right? He produced a weapon that would cause mass destruction all over the world."

"I know," Yousef agreed, "and I got him the funding for it. So, if you think it was him alone, you're wrong. I may not have had the scientific smarts to do what he did, but we were a team, and you did your level best to take out that team. And you did, … everyone but him. And eventually he succumbed. But no way in hell you'll put it behind you. Even if you take me out right now," Yousef said, "and I don't get that chance to live a life that I've always dreamed of, yet I also know that you won't either. Your partner, your child? … They'll be killed before you have a chance to do anything. If I don't make sure of it myself, it still goes down."

"Doesn't matter if it goes down or not," Terk noted. "I trust my team. I trust my brother. I trust my family, and she's not my partner, and she's not carrying my child."

"And you're wrong," Yousef roared in fury. "Why won't you believe me?"

"Why would I?" Terk asked. "Only a DNA test will prove something like that. So I won't listen to any garbage you have to say. You're all liars and cheats."

"We are not!" He fired in Terk's direction.

From the roof across the way, Brody broke into a run, and, coming up on the other side of the gunman, he started shooting.

Yousef took the first one in the chest, and he went down, gasping.

He tried to raise his weapon again, and Brody dropped him with a shot to his knee. "It doesn't have to be this way," Brody called out.

"Of course it does," Yousef replied, with a gurgling laugh. "It still isn't over, but I will have the last laugh."

"Well, it will be over," Brody promised. "Just not the way you had hoped." And, with that, as Yousef finally managed to get his fingers wrapped around the weapon and slowly raised it, Brody put a third bullet right between his eyes. With that done, he raced over to the far wall and checked to see if Damon was okay. Damon lifted a hand and sent out the all-clear notice.

Brody walked back to the edge and said to Terk, "Both snipers down." But Brody saw no sign of Terk. Knowing that their priority was now whatever was going on inside headquarters, he sent out a message to Damon, and they both raced downstairs and headed in. Brody could only hope he got there before anything happened to Clary or the rest of them.

But he also knew it could be damn ugly.

As soon as they broached the door, whoever was inside would be trapped, and they would know it. So it would get ugly right after that.

No one wants to be taken down lightly, and they would want to wreak as much havoc as they can manage.

It was about time to end this mess for good.

CHAPTER 14

W HEN THE BEDROOM door was tried once again, Clary worried at the insistence of whoever was on the other side. She found herself getting damn angry. She went over to the door and flung it open, staring at the man on the other side.

"What?" she asked. "What the hell is your problem?"

He looked at her in surprise and then look behind her at the bed.

"If you wake that little boy up, I'll be pissed."

He started to laugh. "I don't think it makes a damn bit of difference what you feel." He lifted his gun and turned it toward her.

She didn't even think twice and kicked out so the gun dropped from his hand.

The guy looked up at her in anger. "You will pay for this," he roared, as he rushed at her. But she was already out in the hallway, with the door shut on Mariana and Little Calum.

As he raced toward her, she put up an energy wall to stop him dead in his tracks. As soon as he hit that barrier, he stood there vibrating, merely a foot from her, rooted to the spot. He looked stunned.

"What the hell?" he asked, shock in his voice. He reached out a hand, trying to get past the energy barrier she had created.

He shook his head. "God damn witch," he said in a guttural voice, but such animosity filled his tone that she knew he wouldn't leave them alone. He was out for blood, and, if it didn't come from her, it would come from whoever he attacked next.

She looked at him. "No witches here," she murmured. "But I can see that, from your perspective, maybe this is not quite what you thought would happen."

He yelled out, "This shouldn't happen. This is not allowed to happen."

She frowned at him. "I think you forgot to tell somebody then."

The mocking tone of her voice was grating on him, and he was mad.

She bent into a crouch, as her karate instructor had taught her. She wouldn't tell this guy that she was rusty, since her fighting skills were almost nonexistent, but it was all she could do. "Bring it on," she taunted him.

"Do you think you're so mighty? Let's see," he roared and raced at her. Only about six feet stood between them, but, before he ever got there, she had her barrier firmly in place, and, once again he hit it with a crushing blow. He stood there bewildered, not knowing how to approach. It was a first for him, and he knew nothing about how to deal with energy work like this that he had never seen.

She smiled at him. "See? You never should judge a book by its cover," she stated cheerfully. "You cannot touch me."

"No, you're wrong." He pulled a second weapon that had been holstered on his calf. With a small snub-nose revolver facing her now, he glared at her. "Not so brave now, are you?" He was chuckling and clearly back in his element.

She looked at him, seething. "You think that'll stop me?" she murmured. "I don't think so."

He looked at her in astonishment. "Oh, I think it will." He spoke as if to an imbecile. "I get that you think that there's something special about you, but you're nothing, absolutely nothing."

"And you're just a hired gunman," she stated. "I suspect if you were to step outside of this building, some stupid ass behind a drone will take you out."

He laughed. "You are so naïve. Nope. That won't happen. They already took out everybody who needed to be taken out, but that's not me. I'm part of the end game."

"Well, then bring it on, big guy." She tapped into Brody's energy, and he was fine; it was all good. "I don't think you understand, but the end game has already happened. It's already all over on the rooftops." She smirked. "Both snipers are dead."

He glared at her. "You don't know anything, no way."

"I know more than you do," she stated calmly, her gaze on the gun because, regardless of the shield, it still wasn't anything to fool around with. He could shoot her, and, while her sister might save her, there was also a good chance that Cara wouldn't get to Clary in time. Or that Cara was otherwise occupied, trying to save somebody else.

"Someone is on the way here," she told her gunman.

"You're just pissing me off." He looked completely confused by her attitude, as if this was not at all what he'd expected.

"I get it," she explained. "You're looking for somebody to quiver in place and to cry out and to plead for their life. You picked the wrong woman today. No way I'll give you what you want. I've had enough of dealing with shitheads like you."

He glared at her. "Don't you talk to me like that," he roared.

She shrugged. "Or what?" she muttered. "You'll shoot me?"

He raised his gun and fired. Almost instantly it hit the barrier, resulting in a shockwave. She wasn't sure that she would even hold it in place, but still she managed. That just pissed him off that much more. He immediately started firing over and over and over again.

She held the barrier as the bullets dropped at her feet.

"Now I know," he sneered, with a ghostly certainty. "I wasn't so sure you all needed to be killed, but now I do. You should never, ever be allowed to live. This is not normal. *You* are not normal."

"I'm as normal as anyone else," she declared. "You're just the sad sack, sitting here, waiting for something better in life, instead of creating it."

"No, no, no." He looked at the gun in his hand, then back at her. "You don't even have a weapon. How is the world supposed to function when somebody like you is allowed to live? You are an abomination!" he bellowed, then charged right at her. Unfortunately the barrier had been battered enough, and the energy had dissipated already. As soon as he attacked, the rest of it crumpled, and his hands closed around her throat.

All she could do to fight was to call out telepathically for help. She reached out to Brody or anybody who was close. She tried hard to pull the energy in and to knock out the guy hard and fast. But he had a hard grip, and she was already getting weak.

When the door behind her opened, all she wanted was to

warn them to stay inside. She wanted to cry out to tell them to barricade themselves inside. This wasn't something for them to see.

Suddenly energy surged through her fingertips. The surge was so great that she felt almost euphoric. With the pain and struggle gone, she felt a powerful source, giving her the strength she so desperately needed.

She smiled and gave her attacker an energy shock that propelled him backward six feet. He landed on his ass with a *thud*. She walked over and told him, "While we are preaching, some people should not be allowed to live at all."

She reached down, and, while she hated doing it, this was necessary. It was the only way that she could keep everybody safe. Placing a hand on his heart, she said, "Now I suggest you go easy. Go to your Allah because it'll just get much harder for you. I really doubt that you'll be forgiven for the lives that you have taken and ruined."

She slowly but steadily drained all his energy, until nothing was left. He was hanging on by a thread, but she left him alive because it wasn't within her to kill.

When Brody reached her a little bit later and took one look at the guy prone on the floor and obviously what had happened here, he held open his arms, and she rushed into them.

She cried softly against his shoulder. "I'm so glad you're here. I couldn't kill him," she whispered, "I just kind of …"

"It's okay. You're okay. I'm glad to hear it," he said gently against her ear. "There has to be some value to human life. Otherwise we would all kill indiscriminately. That's not what we're here for."

"He was trying to kill me." She looked up at Brody. "He was trying to kill all of us." She felt her hysteria rising.

He nodded. "I know. I really do. Thank you for saving them."

Clary shook her head. "You don't understand. Someone fed me energy to overpower my attacker, just before I feared I would black out." Brody's fear was evident on his face. Clary turned to the bedroom she had been guarding, finding Mariana and Little Calum watching her carefully. "Did you help me?" she asked, facing Mariana, who looked confused. Clary's arms reacted with goose bumps as she turned to Little Calum.

"Was that okay?" he asked.

Clary burst into tears, reaching out to hug the gifted little boy. "It was perfect, Calum. You saved my life. Do you know that?"

"No," he replied innocently. "I saved everybody's."

Clary now laughed, while she cried. "You did, my precious little one. You saved us all." Clary shared her wonder with all those standing around them now. A huge crowd had gathered to hear the exchange. She smiled gently as she looked at everyone, then pointed to the unconscious intruder, anxiously hoping that they wouldn't judge her for it. "He's not dead."

Her sister walked over and gave her a big hug. "He's not dead. You did a good job. You don't need to feel guilty."

"But I do," she said sadly, "but just because we can kill doesn't mean we should."

"No, we absolutely shouldn't," she whispered, holding her close. "You did good, sis."

She looked back at the others, who were smiling and nodding. Brody wrapped his arms around her and whispered, "He is not worth your tears."

"I know it sounds foolish," she said, "but I kind of felt

sorry for him in the end. He really didn't know what he was up against."

Brody smiled. "I have felt that many times," he replied gently. "They never really do. We have an ability that's not generally seen in this world," he explained. "And when we come up against something that we don't know how to handle or, in our case, that we're really good at handling," he continued, "it is almost sad to confront our attackers."

She nodded. "Yet I didn't want him to hurt us or to hurt anybody else." She stepped away, looking at the others, when Mariana walked up.

Wrapping her arms around Clary, Mariana whispered, "Thank you, Clary. Thank you so much."

Clary knew very well what she meant and gently touched the other woman, patting her on the arm.

"Come on now. It's all good," Clary replied. "None of us needed to die today. And definitely not that little guy."

Mariana grinned happily. She gave Clary another big hug and then walked over to scoop up Little Calum. With him in her arms, she joined Cal.

With everybody holding on to each other, Clary smiled at Brody. "So, all's well that ends well?" He shrugged. And that's when it dawned on her. She turned, searching, almost frantically. "Where is he?" she asked.

"Who?" He looked at her steadily.

"Where's Terk?" she demanded.

"He's gone."

"What do you mean, *gone*?" she asked, her voice rising quickly. "Where is he?"

"He's headed to the US," Brody murmured. "His brother already got him tickets, while all this was happening. The plane leaves in like twenty minutes."

"Oh, good God." She stared out frantically into the energy. "He won't make it."

"He'll make it, Clary. That's one thing I am damn sure of."

She shook her head. "Of course you are, but it's not that easy. There are a million rules and regulations these days."

He smiled. "By now you should know that Terk gets to bypass a lot of that," Brody noted quietly. "What we have to do now is everything we can to make sure that we survive. He'll be okay."

She stared out again, feeling lost. "I don't … I don't even know what to say." She turned to look at her sister, who didn't appear alarmed at all.

"I know," Cara said. "We can check on him together."

They merged their energy to look for Terk and located him at once. He recoiled from their touch and immediately disconnected from their energy. It was like an immediate loss.

"See? He's out there, and he's safe." Cara tried to reassure her sister.

"For now," Clary admitted, "but surely you felt that pain and anger. He's detaching," she said, alarmed. "And I don't like that at all."

"He'll do whatever he needs to do to keep his family safe," Cara replied softly.

And, with that, Brody clued them in on everything that had happened while they were up on the roof.

"Does he believe it's his child that Celia's carrying?" Clary stared at Brody in surprise. "Or is it really a bluff?"

"Terk believes it," Damon confirmed from her side. "And, if not, he's not leaving it to chance."

Clary frowned, thinking about that. "But it could be a

trap."

"No, not *could* be," Brody stated. "It's definitely a trap. And everybody at Levi's compound knows it. Some of us will go after him to help him out."

"He got a chance at an immediate flight out, and we told him to go," Damon added.

Clary nodded slowly. "I guess that makes sense, but wow," she murmured. "It's not what I expected at all."

"No, of course not," Brody said. "You may have thought he'd be here doing a victory dance with the rest of us. But, in his case, it's not yet a victory."

"Dear God," Clary murmured. "I can't bear the thought of my family getting hurt."

"You also know that plenty of assholes are out there in this world, who are always thinking about how to bring down Terk. They've got a plan in play all ready for Celia and her child and Merk, plus our team and Levi and Ice's team as well," Brody reminded her. "So Terk'll do everything he can to put a stop to it."

Clary just stared at him. "He can't do it alone."

"Well, he's got us, and some of us will go, like we just said," Brody murmured. "But, more than that, Terk also has his brother and a whole team that will do anything for him. He's kept us all alive many times over this year alone, and he's part of our family."

She nodded slowly. "Maybe, but it still feels wrong." She looked around at her sister. "What's your take on it?"

"It's wrong," Cara stated immediately. She glanced around at the group. "I'm not sure how many we can spare, but, as many as can leave, they should get going right now."

They looked around at each other for a moment, then Cara spoke again.

"Damon, you should go."

"Sure, but any particular reason?"

"I don't know," Cara admitted. "All I can tell you is that you need to go. As many of the team as we can safely spare." She looked at Brody, then shook her head. "Not you."

BRODY SNORTED. "WHAT'S wrong with me?" he snapped.

"You are still hurt," Clary stated, "and your energy won't improve if you hop on a plane to fight the demons of this nightmare. You have to stay put, so no transatlantic flight for you."

"What will I do?" Brody asked, not liking Clary's answer at all.

"You'll stay behind and look after the rest of us."

He just glared at her, not sure how to argue something that he knew was right. He couldn't possibly win this fight.

She looked at him and smiled. "We will fight on the sidelines. It's not bad. You'll see," Clary stated. "It is not a bad idea in the least to have you here, fighting with us."

He groaned. "But the action will be on the other side of the ocean."

She nodded. "It absolutely will, but not for you."

And there wasn't anything he could say that would sway either of the twins. By the time the dust had settled, the rest of the team had gone stateside, and they still hadn't heard from Terk.

As Brody walked into her bedroom later and sat down on the edge of her bed, where Clary was curled under a blanket, he asked, "Have you contacted Terk?"

"Multiple times."

"I've also left a message for him to check in with us."

"He knows, and he will as soon as he can."

Brody swore softly. "But what if he can't?"

"Then it's the same as it is for all of us," Clary noted quietly. "Decisions will have to be made, but I think it's way too early for that yet," she murmured. "He's probably shutting down in order to preserve his energy. He also has to come up with some kind of a game plan, and I don't know how he makes decisions as to what he's doing in his life, but, now more than ever, he's got to make the right decision."

"Of course he will," Brody declared. "Terk is really special."

"He is, indeed," she agreed, "and that's why all of us want to see him thrive in this situation. However, right now, things are dicey, and it might get ugly."

"Of course it will," he said sadly. "When it comes to this kind of shit, ugly is what we do."

She smiled. "I know that, and that's a really good point about trusting in him and the team to handle what we've got coming."

He nodded. "How did you get to be so smart?"

"That's easy," she replied, with a bright smile. "*Experience*. I've seen what men can do to each other. I'm always rooting on the side of right. So, even though it might be a long haul, we'll be fine."

"You promise?" Brody stared at her steadily.

"I do not have the gift of foresight," she noted. "But, as far as I'm concerned, I'll be just fine."

He nodded slowly. "Good. I hope so. I sure don't want anything to go wrong at this point. It took us all to get here, and we've got another chance," he said.

"Speaking of second chances," she replied, "how are you

doing?"

"I'm feeling good," he said, changing the subject.

She smiled and nodded at him. "Maybe you should get some sleep."

"Well, I was thinking of bed," he noted, "but I'm not so sure about *sleep*."

CHAPTER 15

C LARY'D BEEN WONDERING when this stage would come but had deliberately not put any energy into seeking answers. Some things just had to happen on their own, and sometimes things just never did. She sucked in her breath. "Isn't that a little sudden?"

"I don't think it's sudden at all," he declared. "I might be dense but not dense forever."

She snorted at that. "Glad you told me," she teased. "I might not have figured that out without your added insights."

He rolled his eyes at her. "I get it. I was pretty aloof. I was pretty foolish, and I just didn't get it."

"Nope, you sure didn't." She smiled up at him. "And I'm not sure you even do now."

"No, I probably don't," he murmured, "but I get a whole lot more than I did before."

"Good. So just what is it you understand?"

"That we are bonded," he said, "in some ways. Maybe to the point where we have to agree to transcend in a way that is beyond the understanding of this whole universe."

"How did you come to that conclusion?"

"When I feel your energy lighting me up, I am almost ecstatic," he shared, "and feel such a familiarity to it."

"Of course, but I was helping you while you were under," she murmured. "So it may just be infatuation. Maybe it's not anything more. Maybe all you want is something familiar."

He smiled. "Oh no you don't. … You don't get off that easy."

She raised an eyebrow. "Really? Maybe you should tell me more."

"I could, … or I could show you."

"What does sex have to do with anything?" she asked in a lighthearted tone.

"It doesn't have anything to do with anything except for a beautiful pastime," he explained, "particularly when two people care about each other."

Her heart heard almost everything that she wanted to hear, but she also looked for that acknowledgment, something special, something different from what he was doing so far. Lacking that made her uneasy.

The last thing she wanted was to fall for someone who didn't quite get it. She didn't want to disappoint both of them. She wanted him to get it right, before they moved on to the next step.

And, of course, that was her, demanding what was hardly fair. She knew it wasn't fair, but it had to be right.

"I look at your face, and I realize that you're still insecure," Brody noted.

"Any reason why I shouldn't be?" She stared at him. "I mean, it's not as if this has been a particularly smooth road so far, has it?"

"No, it hasn't been smooth at all," he agreed regretfully. "And I'm sorry for that. Yet it doesn't even feel like we've been separated since I woke up."

"We haven't been," she stated. "Is that a problem?"

"Not for me," he replied, "but it might be for you. I'm not sure how much space you'll get in this wacky place we have for a home."

"Tasha said the main team disappears all the damn time," Clary shared, "and that will ease up the space and togetherness issue."

Brody smiled. "And how about down the road? Will you be okay with that being part of our new life?"

"Our new life?" she asked, with a note of amusement. "You do know I'll go off and still do other jobs, right?"

"I hope so," he said, "and I hope that, when somebody here needs you, you'll be here for them too."

Thankfully he had moved on to the right territory.

"You have a gift, Clary. One that I had no idea was even possible, but just working with Terk has opened up a world that I didn't know existed. Now I realize that your powers are almost on the same level as Terk's."

"Really?"

"Yes. I honestly have no idea what to say to you, but you have a special gift, and I would never keep you from your job. I'm sorry it took me some time, but I didn't even know you. Even now I'm still—what do they say here?— *gobsmacked* about it."

At that phrase, she burst out laughing. "Well, that's one way to think of it."

He grinned at her. "I don't know about that, but I do know that we need some time together to figure out who and what we are. More important, what we are to each other," he explained. "I feel like I already know who you are on the inside, but I really don't know a whole lot about you—like your favorite foods and your favorite colors and your favorite music."

She closed her eyes and opened the connection that had always existed between them. "How do you feel about that?"

He stared at her in surprise and repeated, "Mozart?" Then he stopped, looking at her in awe at what she could do. "So, you like classical, *huh*?"

She burst out laughing. "Anything else you feel like we don't know about each other?"

"I feel like, … in a way, that I can't live without you." Then he stopped and stared at her. "Does that make sense?"

"It does in our case," she noted. "When I said I had to go deep to save your life, I meant it. But by letting myself go deep, I also had to give of myself, and then, when you didn't seem to even want the gift there waiting for you—"

"*Shhh.*" He'd reached out and placed a finger over her lips. "I was an idiot," he murmured. "You can't hold it against me."

She looked at him in surprise. "Why not?"

"Because I wasn't myself," he said automatically. "And now I'm really looking forward to the future, figuring out what we can do and how this all works."

She laughed. "Sounds like an experiment."

"Nope, not an experiment," he disagreed. "How about a homecoming?"

At that, her breath caught in the back of her throat. "You know that … sounds pretty decent," she said in a soft tone. "Something I've always wanted …"

"What?" he asked. "A homecoming?"

"Maybe more like a partner."

"I don't think either of us ever really expected to get a partner like this," Brody stated, as he leaned over and ever-so-gently lifted her chin and kissed her on the lips.

At first, he was just testing the waters, as if figuring out who this person was—who was already half of his heart. "It's such an odd thing," he murmured. "I know so much, and yet I don't know anything."

"It's called the age of exploration," she murmured. "We have lots of time to fill in the blanks."

"Maybe, but some of the blanks I really want to fill in right now." And he gathered her up in his arms, and this time he kissed her passionately. Instead of just testing the waters, he let go of any reservations.

As in, all or nothing.

The heat was intense, like a fire running through his veins—a passion that flew through them. And there was also the sense of rightness, the sense of coming home.

She opened her arms, then she opened the door between their thoughts a little bit wider, so he could feel the feelings flowing through her, as they always could when she was connected to him.

He pulled back in astonishment. "Oh my God." He then lowered his head to kiss her with so much passion and so much enjoyment that she realized he was finally getting the message.

This really was the extent of their merger, all the raw passion and power and energy available to them. All they had to do was reach out and make it happen. But it had to happen on an energy level; it couldn't just happen on the physical plane.

He was absolutely submerged in a sea of emotions, showing absolutely no hesitation, as he swept her up and quickly stood her on her feet and threw back the blankets. By the time he turned back around again she stood before him, naked.

He stared at her in shock. "That's much better. ... I

don't know how you managed to do that so damn fast, but I'm impressed."

"I don't know why, since I dressed pretty simply." She stepped forward and quickly pulled his T-shirt up over his head. "Besides, I didn't want to waste time."

Again he paused, then looked at her and shrugged. "If you knew this was coming, and you didn't run, I'm good with that."

She chuckled. "Why would I run? My heart has always known where it belongs." He sucked in his breath, and she saw the emotions working on his features, as he tried to control himself. "Again you're trying to control something that you can't control because it's already loose. Let it be free here." And she tapped his heart.

He groaned and wrapped her up in his arms and proceeded to show her exactly how he felt. Not that she needed additional confirmation, since it was so very wonderful to have the same emotions flowing through her. It was like they were one and the same.

Finally she felt them merge, until there was nothing left to distinguish one from another. As he slowly entered her for the first time, he whispered, "I've never felt anything like this before."

"And you probably won't ever again," she murmured, holding him close.

"This isn't just special," he said, at a loss for words for a moment, "it's magical."

"Maybe it is," she agreed.

"I didn't think it was possible."

"I don't want to talk right now. We're both here. It's perfect. I want this to be just us."

When he entered all the way, her body arched beneath

him, and she cried out, in pain and pleasure. He was already moving, taking her to the next level, quickly pushing her toward the edge. When he followed her, gasping and crying out, she whispered, "What's the rush?"

"I been waiting for this for a very long time. And very soon we will do it your way."

She chuckled and held him close, wrapping her arms around his neck. She whispered in his ears over and over and over.

He held her tight. "I think I've died and gone to heaven."

"Maybe so, because honestly? That is where I found you."

He was surprised for a moment, then opened his mouth as if to say something. Instead he shook his head and wrapped her up close. "Nope, I won't even ask."

"Good."

"Just so you know, if … if I return there," he said, "make sure you drag me back. I don't want to miss one second of our life together."

"Ditto," she said. "You can do the same for me."

He held her even closer and whispered, "I like the sound of that." He kissed her gently on the forehead. "Relax and rest now," he said. "We have the rest of our lives together. And luckily we have the whole night together, uninterrupted."

They closed their eyes and slept, knowing the night was far from over.

EPILOGUE

T HE TRIP TO Texas was brutal. The flight long, noisy, and tedious, when so much in Terk's life was on hold. He'd sent out probes, checking on everyone multiple times, and everyone was fine. Even with that reassurance it was hard for him to relax.

While his brother was at his side, a rare moment for the two of them, it was hard knowing what was coming and what they'd left behind.

"Have you told them where we are?" Merk asked him.

Terk nodded. "Yes, but I've also slowed the energy going to them, so I'll call them when we land."

Merk shook his head but remained silent; then out of the blue, he said, "You know that, even though I'm used to this, it still sounds bizarre what you're saying."

Not much Terk could say to that. His brother had long been his biggest supporter, but that adaptation couldn't have been easy. Terk had often wondered if there was something Merk couldn't tap into or ignored willfully or subconsciously all these years. In Terk's case, his extra senses dominated. Ignoring them wasn't even possible.

"What are you and your team going to do when this is over?" Merk murmured, looking out the plane window. "We're almost there."

"I know, and I've spent much of this flight resting, letting the energy flow in the direction it needs to, and it heads to England every time."

Merk stared at him sharply. "As in a permanent location? As in the entire team or just yourself?"

"Yes, as to location and as in the whole team, including all the new members."

"And Celia?"

That was a question Terk couldn't answer. No one could at this stage. He could see bits and pieces, images that were both dark and intense, yet sprinkled in between softer ones. He knew Celia was important, but the jury was out as to whether she was on the plus side or the minus side. Terk could only hope that, given what he did know, she wasn't involved in the making of this nightmare. If she was, good luck keeping his son away from him. If she wasn't involved in that way, then Terk knew the future would get very interesting, very soon.

The seat belt sign kicked on.

Merk looked over at him and smiled. "You ready? To meet Celia? To see what the hell is going on at this end?"

"Always," Terk murmured, looking at the approaching runway. "And more than ready to end this. Whatever the hell *this* is …"

This concludes Book 7 of Terkel's Team: Brody's Beast.
Read about Terkel's Twist: Terkel's Team, Book 8

Terkel's Team: Terkel's Twist (Book #8)

Welcome to a brand-new series from *USA Today* best-selling author Dale Mayer, where dark-ops SEALs have special senses and skills, needed to solve intrigue, betrayal, and ... murder. A series with all the elements you've come to love, plus so much more, ... including psychics!

In advance of another major attack, Terk races to Levi's compound in Texas, where Terk finally gets to meet Celia, the woman carrying his child. Thankfully he arrives in time to protect his friends and new family from another attack, but he's determined to get to the end of this nightmare that tried to earlier destroy his team.

Finally meeting this stranger—whose child Celia may be carrying—how could she not be suspicious? But after meeting Terk, she believes he had nothing to do with her pregnancy. Only after some deep conversations, as they peel layer from layer, do possible answers surface.

When the pieces finally come together into the most probably theory, Terk realizes how simple this whole mess really is. But solving it? … That's a whole different story.

Find Book 8 here!
To find out more visit Dale Mayer's website.
https://geni.us/DMTTTwistUniversal

Magnus: Shadow Recon (Book #1)

Deep in the permafrost of the Arctic, a joint task force, comprised of over one dozen countries, comes together to level up their winter skills. A mix of personalities, nationalities, and egos bring out the best—and the worst—as these globally elite men and women work and play together. They rub elbows with hardy locals and a group of scientists gathered close by …

One fatality is almost expected with this training. A second is tough but not a surprise. However, when a third goes missing? It's hard to not be suspicious. When the missing man is connected to one of the elite Maverick team members and is a special friend of Lieutenant Commander Mason Callister? All hell breaks loose …

L IEUTENANT COMMANDER MASON Callister walked into the private office and stood in front of retired Navy Commander Doran Magellan.

"Mason, good to see you."

Yet the dry tone of voice, and the scowl pinching the silver-haired man, all belied his words. Mason had known Doran for over a decade, and their friendship had only grown over time.

Mason waited, as he watched the other man try to work the new tech phone system on his desk. With his hand circling the air above the black box, he appeared to hit buttons randomly.

Mason held back his amusement but to no avail.

"Why can't a phone be a phone anymore?" the commander snapped, as his glare shifted from Mason to the box and back.

Asking the commander if he needed help wouldn't make the older man feel any better, but sitting here and watching as he indiscriminately punched buttons was a struggle. "Is Helen away?" Mason asked.

"Yes, damn it. She's at lunch, and I need her to be at lunch." The commander's piercing gaze pinned Mason in place. "No one is to know you're here."

Solemn, Mason nodded. "Understood."

"Doran? Is that you?" A crotchety voice slammed into the room through the phone's speakers. "Get away from that damn phone. You keep clicking buttons in my ear. Get

Helen in there to do this."

"No, she can't be here for this."

Silence came first, then a huge groan. "Damn it. Then you should have connected me last, so I don't have to sit here and listen to you fumbling around."

"Go pour yourself a damn drink then," Doran barked. "I'm working on the others."

A snort was his only response.

Mason bit the inside of his lip, as he really tried to hold back his grin. The retired commander had been hell on wheels while on active duty, and, even now, the retired part of his life seemed to be more of a euphemism than anything.

"Damn things …"

Mason looked around the dark mahogany office and the walls filled with photos, awards, medals. A life of purpose, accomplishment. And all of that had only piqued his interest during the initial call he'd received, telling him to be here at this time.

"Ah, got it."

Mason's eyebrows barely twitched, as the commander gave him a feral grin. "I'd rather lead a warship into battle than deal with some of today's technology."

As he was one of only a few commanders who'd been in a position to do such a thing, it said much about his capabilities.

And much about current technology.

The commander leaned back in his massive chair and motioned to the cart beside Mason. "Pour three cups."

Interesting. Mason walked a couple steps across the rich tapestry-style carpet and lifted the silver service to pour coffee into three very down-to-earth-looking mugs.

"Black for me."

Mason picked up two cups and walked one over to Doran.

"Thanks." He leaned forward and snapped into the phone, "Everyone here?"

Multiple voices responded.

Curiouser and curiouser. Mason recognized several of the voices. Other relics of an era gone by. Although not a one would like to hear that, and, in good faith, it wasn't fair. Mason had thought each of these men were retired, had relinquished power. Yet, as he studied Doran in front of him, Mason had to wonder if any of them actually had passed the baton or if they'd only slid into the shadows. Was this planned with the government's authority? Or were these retirees a shadow group to the government?

The tangible sense of power and control oozed from Doran's words, tone, stature—his very pores. This man might be heading into his sunset years—based on a simple calculation of chronological years spent on the planet—but he was a long way from being out of the action.

"Mason …" Doran began.

"Sir?"

"We've got a problem."

Mason narrowed his gaze and waited.

Doran's glare was hard, steely hard, with an icy glint. "Do you know the Mavericks?"

Mason's eyebrows shot up. The black ops division was one of those well-kept secrets, so, therefore, everyone knew about it. He gave a decisive nod. "I do."

"And you're involved in the logistics behind the ICE training program in the Arctic, are you not?"

"I am." Now where was the commander going with this?

"Do you know another SEAL by the name of Mountain

Rode? He's been working for the black ops Mavericks." At his own words, the commander shook his head. "What the hell was his mother thinking when she gave him that moniker?"

"She wasn't thinking anything," said the man with a hard voice from behind Mason.

He stiffened slightly, then relaxed as he recognized that voice too.

"She died giving birth to me. And my full legal name is Mountain Bear Rode. It was my father's doing."

The commander glared at the new arrival. "Did I say you could come in?"

"Yes." Mountain's voice was firm, yet a definitive note of affection filled his tone.

That emotion told Mason so much.

The commander harrumphed, then cleared his throat. "Mason, we're picking up a significant amount of chatter over that ICE training. Most of it good. Some of it the usual caterwauling we've come to expect every time we participate in a joint training mission. This one is set to run for six months, then to reassess."

Mason already knew this. But he waited for the commander to get around to why Mason was here, and, more important, what any of this had to do with the mountain of a man who now towered beside him.

The commander shifted his gaze to Mountain, but he remained silent.

Mason noted Mountain was not only physically big but damn imposing and severely pissed, seemingly barely holding back the forces within. His body language seemed to yell, *And the world will fix this, or I'll find the reason why.*

For a moment Mason felt sorry for the world.

Finally a voice spoke through the phone. "Mason, this is Alpha here. I run the Mavericks. We've got a problem with that ICE training center. Mountain, tell him."

Mason shifted to include Mountain in his field of vision. Mason wished the other men on the conference call were in the room too. It was one thing to deal with men you knew and could take the measure of; it was another when they were silent shadows in the background.

"My brother is one of the men who reported for the Artic training three weeks ago."

"Tergan Rode?" Mason confirmed. "I'm the one who arranged for him to go up there. He's a great kid."

A glimmer of a smile cracked Mountain's stony features. He nodded. "Indeed. A bright light in my often dark world. He's a dozen years younger than me, just passed his BUD/s training this spring, and raring to go. Until his raring to go then got up and went."

Oh, shit. Mason's gaze zinged to the commander, who had kicked up his feet to rest atop the big desk. Stocking feet. With Mickey Mouse images dancing on them. Sidetracked, Mason struggled to pull his attention back to Mountain. "Meaning?"

"He's disappeared." Mountain let out a harsh breath, as if just saying that out loud, and maybe to the right people, could allow him to relax—at least a little.

The commander spoke up. "We need your help, Mason. You're uniquely qualified for this problem."

It didn't sound like he was qualified in any way for anything he'd heard so far. "Clarify." His spoken word was simplicity itself, but the tone behind it said he wanted the cards on the table … now.

Mountain spoke up. "He's the third incident."

Mason's gaze narrowed, as the reports from the training

camp rolled through his mind. "One was Russian. One was from the German SEAL team. Both were deemed accidental deaths."

"No, they weren't."

There it was. The root of the problem in black-and-white. He studied Mountain, aiming for neutrality. "Do you have evidence?"

"My brother did."

"Ah, hell."

Mountain gave a clipped nod. "I'm going to find him."

"Of that I have no doubt," Mason said quietly. "Do you have a copy of the evidence he collected?"

"I have some of it." Mountain held out a USB key. "This is your copy. Top secret."

"We don't have to remind you, Mason, that lives are at stake," Doran added. "Nor do we need another international incident. Consider also that a group of scientists, studying global warming, is close by, and not too far away is a village home to a few hardy locals."

Mason accepted the key, turned to the commander, and asked, "Do we know if this is internal or enemy warfare?"

"We don't know at this point," Alpha replied through the phone. "Mountain will lead Shadow Recon. His mission is twofold. One, find out what's behind these so-called accidents and put a stop to it by any means necessary. Two, locate his brother, hopefully alive."

"And where do I come in?" Mason asked.

"We want you to pull together a special team. The members of Shadow Recon will report to both you and Mountain, just in case."

That was clear enough.

"You'll stay stateside but in constant communication with Mountain—with the caveat that, if necessary, you're on the next flight out."

"What about bringing in other members from the Mavericks?" Mason suggested.

Alpha took this question too, his response coming through via Speakerphone. "We don't have the numbers. The budget for our division has been cut. So we called the commander to pull some strings."

That was Doran's cue to explain further. "Mountain has fought hard to get me on board with this plan, and I'm here now. The navy has a special budget for Shadow Recon and will take care of Mountain and you, Mason, and the team you provide."

"Skills needed?"

"Everything," Mountain said, his voice harsh. "But the biggest is these men need to operate in the shadows, mostly alone, without a team beside them. Too many new arrivals will alert the enemy. If we make any changes to the training program, it will raise alarms. We'll move the men in one or two at a time on the same rotation that the trainees are running right now."

"And when we get to the bottom of this?" Mason looked from the commander back to Mountain.

"Then the training can resume as usual," Doran stated.

Mason immediately churned through the names already popping up in his mind. How much could he tell his men? Obviously not much. Hell, he didn't know much himself. How much time did he have? "Timeline?"

The commander's final word told him of the urgency.

"Yesterday."

Find Magnus here!

To find out more visit Dale Mayer's website.

https://geni.us/DMSRMagnusUniversal

Author's Note

Thank you for reading Brody's Beast: Terkel's Team, Book 7! If you enjoyed the book, please take a moment and leave a short review.

Dear reader,

I love to hear from readers, and you can contact me at my website: www.dalemayer.com or at my Facebook author page. To be informed of new releases and special offers, sign up for my newsletter or follow me on BookBub. And if you are interested in joining Dale Mayer's Reader Group, here is the Facebook sign up page.
http://geni.us/DaleMayerFBGroup

Cheers,
Dale Mayer

Get THREE Free Books Now!

Have you met the SEALS of Honor?

SEALs of Honor Books 1, 2, and 3. Follow the stories of brave, badass warriors who serve their country with honor and love their women to the limits of life and death.

Read Mason, Hawk, and Dane right now for FREE.

Go here and tell me where to send them!
https://dalemayer.com/masonfree

About the Author

Dale Mayer is a *USA Today* best-selling author, best known for her SEALs military romances, her Psychic Visions series, and her Lovely Lethal Garden cozy series. Her contemporary romances are raw and full of passion and emotion (Broken But … Mending, Hathaway House series). Her thrillers will keep you guessing (Kate Morgan, By Death series), and her romantic comedies will keep you giggling (*It's a Dog's Life*, a stand-alone novella; and the Broken Protocols series, starring Charming Marvin, the cat).

Dale honors the stories that come to her—and some of them are crazy, break all the rules and cross multiple genres!

To go with her fiction, she also writes nonfiction in many different fields, with books available on résumé writing, companion gardening, and the US mortgage system. All her books are available in print and ebook format.

Connect with Dale Mayer Online

Dale's Website – www.dalemayer.com
Twitter – @DaleMayer
Facebook Page – geni.us/DaleMayerFBFanPage
Facebook Group – geni.us/DaleMayerFBGroup
BookBub – geni.us/DaleMayerBookbub
Instagram – geni.us/DaleMayerInstagram
Goodreads – geni.us/DaleMayerGoodreads
Newsletter – geni.us/DaleNews

Also by Dale Mayer

Published Adult Books:

Shadow Recon
Magnus, Book 1

Bullard's Battle
Ryland's Reach, Book 1
Cain's Cross, Book 2
Eton's Escape, Book 3
Garret's Gambit, Book 4
Kano's Keep, Book 5
Fallon's Flaw, Book 6
Quinn's Quest, Book 7
Bullard's Beauty, Book 8
Bullard's Best, Book 9
Bullard's Battle, Books 1–2
Bullard's Battle, Books 3–4
Bullard's Battle, Books 5–6
Bullard's Battle, Books 7–8

Terkel's Team
Damon's Deal, Book 1
Wade's War, Book 2
Gage's Goal, Book 3
Calum's Contact, Book 4
Rick's Road, Book 5

Scott's Summit, Book 6
Brody's Beast, Book 7
Terkel's Twist, Book 8

Kate Morgan
Simon Says… Hide, Book 1
Simon Says… Jump, Book 2
Simon Says… Ride, Book 3
Simon Says… Scream, Book 4
Simon Says… Run, Book 5

Hathaway House
Aaron, Book 1
Brock, Book 2
Cole, Book 3
Denton, Book 4
Elliot, Book 5
Finn, Book 6
Gregory, Book 7
Heath, Book 8
Iain, Book 9
Jaden, Book 10
Keith, Book 11
Lance, Book 12
Melissa, Book 13
Nash, Book 14
Owen, Book 15
Percy, Book 16
Quinton, Book 17
Ryatt, Book 18
Hathaway House, Books 1–3
Hathaway House, Books 4–6

Hathaway House, Books 7–9

The K9 Files
Ethan, Book 1
Pierce, Book 2
Zane, Book 3
Blaze, Book 4
Lucas, Book 5
Parker, Book 6
Carter, Book 7
Weston, Book 8
Greyson, Book 9
Rowan, Book 10
Caleb, Book 11
Kurt, Book 12
Tucker, Book 13
Harley, Book 14
Kyron, Book 15
Jenner, Book 16
Rhys, Book 17
Landon, Book 18
The K9 Files, Books 1–2
The K9 Files, Books 3–4
The K9 Files, Books 5–6
The K9 Files, Books 7–8
The K9 Files, Books 9–10
The K9 Files, Books 11–12

Lovely Lethal Gardens
Arsenic in the Azaleas, Book 1
Bones in the Begonias, Book 2
Corpse in the Carnations, Book 3

Daggers in the Dahlias, Book 4
Evidence in the Echinacea, Book 5
Footprints in the Ferns, Book 6
Gun in the Gardenias, Book 7
Handcuffs in the Heather, Book 8
Ice Pick in the Ivy, Book 9
Jewels in the Juniper, Book 10
Killer in the Kiwis, Book 11
Lifeless in the Lilies, Book 12
Murder in the Marigolds, Book 13
Nabbed in the Nasturtiums, Book 14
Offed in the Orchids, Book 15
Poison in the Pansies, Book 16
Quarry in the Quince, Book 17
Revenge in the Roses, Book 18
Silenced in the Sunflowers, Book 19
Lovely Lethal Gardens, Books 1–2
Lovely Lethal Gardens, Books 3–4
Lovely Lethal Gardens, Books 5–6
Lovely Lethal Gardens, Books 7–8
Lovely Lethal Gardens, Books 9–10

Psychic Vision Series
Tuesday's Child
Hide 'n Go Seek
Maddy's Floor
Garden of Sorrow
Knock Knock…
Rare Find
Eyes to the Soul
Now You See Her
Shattered

Into the Abyss
Seeds of Malice
Eye of the Falcon
Itsy-Bitsy Spider
Unmasked
Deep Beneath
From the Ashes
Stroke of Death
Ice Maiden
Snap, Crackle…
What If…
Talking Bones
String of Tears
Psychic Visions Books 1–3
Psychic Visions Books 4–6
Psychic Visions Books 7–9

By Death Series
Touched by Death
Haunted by Death
Chilled by Death
By Death Books 1–3

Broken Protocols – Romantic Comedy Series
Cat's Meow
Cat's Pajamas
Cat's Cradle
Cat's Claus
Broken Protocols 1-4

Broken and… Mending
Skin

Scars
Scales (of Justice)
Broken but… Mending 1-3

Glory

Genesis
Tori
Celeste
Glory Trilogy

Biker Blues

Morgan: Biker Blues, Volume 1
Cash: Biker Blues, Volume 2

SEALs of Honor

Mason: SEALs of Honor, Book 1
Hawk: SEALs of Honor, Book 2
Dane: SEALs of Honor, Book 3
Swede: SEALs of Honor, Book 4
Shadow: SEALs of Honor, Book 5
Cooper: SEALs of Honor, Book 6
Markus: SEALs of Honor, Book 7
Evan: SEALs of Honor, Book 8
Mason's Wish: SEALs of Honor, Book 9
Chase: SEALs of Honor, Book 10
Brett: SEALs of Honor, Book 11
Devlin: SEALs of Honor, Book 12
Easton: SEALs of Honor, Book 13
Ryder: SEALs of Honor, Book 14
Macklin: SEALs of Honor, Book 15
Corey: SEALs of Honor, Book 16
Warrick: SEALs of Honor, Book 17

Tanner: SEALs of Honor, Book 18
Jackson: SEALs of Honor, Book 19
Kanen: SEALs of Honor, Book 20
Nelson: SEALs of Honor, Book 21
Taylor: SEALs of Honor, Book 22
Colton: SEALs of Honor, Book 23
Troy: SEALs of Honor, Book 24
Axel: SEALs of Honor, Book 25
Baylor: SEALs of Honor, Book 26
Hudson: SEALs of Honor, Book 27
Lachlan: SEALs of Honor, Book 28
Paxton: SEALs of Honor, Book 29
SEALs of Honor, Books 1–3
SEALs of Honor, Books 4–6
SEALs of Honor, Books 7–10
SEALs of Honor, Books 11–13
SEALs of Honor, Books 14–16
SEALs of Honor, Books 17–19
SEALs of Honor, Books 20–22
SEALs of Honor, Books 23–25

Heroes for Hire

Levi's Legend: Heroes for Hire, Book 1
Stone's Surrender: Heroes for Hire, Book 2
Merk's Mistake: Heroes for Hire, Book 3
Rhodes's Reward: Heroes for Hire, Book 4
Flynn's Firecracker: Heroes for Hire, Book 5
Logan's Light: Heroes for Hire, Book 6
Harrison's Heart: Heroes for Hire, Book 7
Saul's Sweetheart: Heroes for Hire, Book 8
Dakota's Delight: Heroes for Hire, Book 9
Tyson's Treasure: Heroes for Hire, Book 10

Jace's Jewel: Heroes for Hire, Book 11
Rory's Rose: Heroes for Hire, Book 12
Brandon's Bliss: Heroes for Hire, Book 13
Liam's Lily: Heroes for Hire, Book 14
North's Nikki: Heroes for Hire, Book 15
Anders's Angel: Heroes for Hire, Book 16
Reyes's Raina: Heroes for Hire, Book 17
Dezi's Diamond: Heroes for Hire, Book 18
Vince's Vixen: Heroes for Hire, Book 19
Ice's Icing: Heroes for Hire, Book 20
Johan's Joy: Heroes for Hire, Book 21
Galen's Gemma: Heroes for Hire, Book 22
Zack's Zest: Heroes for Hire, Book 23
Bonaparte's Belle: Heroes for Hire, Book 24
Noah's Nemesis: Heroes for Hire, Book 25
Tomas's Trials: Heroes for Hire, Book 26
Carson's Choice: Heroes for Hire, Book 27
Dante's Decision: Heroes for Hire, Book 28
Heroes for Hire, Books 1–3
Heroes for Hire, Books 4–6
Heroes for Hire, Books 7–9
Heroes for Hire, Books 10–12
Heroes for Hire, Books 13–15
Heroes for Hire, Books 16–18
Heroes for Hire, Books 19–21
Heroes for Hire, Books 22–24

SEALs of Steel
Badger: SEALs of Steel, Book 1
Erick: SEALs of Steel, Book 2
Cade: SEALs of Steel, Book 3
Talon: SEALs of Steel, Book 4

Laszlo: SEALs of Steel, Book 5
Geir: SEALs of Steel, Book 6
Jager: SEALs of Steel, Book 7
The Final Reveal: SEALs of Steel, Book 8
SEALs of Steel, Books 1–4
SEALs of Steel, Books 5–8
SEALs of Steel, Books 1–8

The Mavericks

Kerrick, Book 1
Griffin, Book 2
Jax, Book 3
Beau, Book 4
Asher, Book 5
Ryker, Book 6
Miles, Book 7
Nico, Book 8
Keane, Book 9
Lennox, Book 10
Gavin, Book 11
Shane, Book 12
Diesel, Book 13
Jerricho, Book 14
Killian, Book 15
Hatch, Book 16
Corbin, Book 17
Aiden, Book 18
The Mavericks, Books 1–2
The Mavericks, Books 3–4
The Mavericks, Books 5–6
The Mavericks, Books 7–8
The Mavericks, Books 9–10

The Mavericks, Books 11–12

Collections
Dare to Be You…
Dare to Love…
Dare to be Strong…
RomanceX3

Standalone Novellas
It's a Dog's Life
Riana's Revenge
Second Chances

Published Young Adult Books:

Family Blood Ties Series
Vampire in Denial
Vampire in Distress
Vampire in Design
Vampire in Deceit
Vampire in Defiance
Vampire in Conflict
Vampire in Chaos
Vampire in Crisis
Vampire in Control
Vampire in Charge
Family Blood Ties Set 1–3
Family Blood Ties Set 1–5
Family Blood Ties Set 4–6
Family Blood Ties Set 7–9
Sian's Solution, A Family Blood Ties Series Prequel
    Novelette

Design series
Dangerous Designs
Deadly Designs
Darkest Designs
Design Series Trilogy

Standalone
In Cassie's Corner
Gem Stone (a Gemma Stone Mystery)
Time Thieves

Published Non-Fiction Books:

Career Essentials
Career Essentials: The Résumé
Career Essentials: The Cover Letter
Career Essentials: The Interview
Career Essentials: 3 in 1

Made in United States
North Haven, CT
22 April 2023

35748601R00141